Lauren's Line

Lauren's Line

Sondra Spatt Olsen

University Press of Mississippi   Jackson

www.upress.state.ms.us

Lauren's Line is a work of fiction. Names, characters,
incidents, and places are fictitious or are used ficti-
tiously. The characters are products of the author's
imagination and do not represent any actual persons.

The University Press of Mississippi is a member
of the Association of American University Presses.

Manufactured in the United States of America
06   05   04   4   3   2   1

Library of Congress Cataloging-in-Publication Data
Olsen, Sondra Spatt, 1936–
 Lauren's line / Sondra Spatt Olsen.
    p. cm.
 ISBN 1-57806-614-X (alk. paper)
 1. English philology—Study and teaching (Higher)—
Fiction. 2. Universities and colleges—Fiction. 3.
College teachers—Fiction. 4. English teachers—Fiction.
I. Title.
PS3565.L79L38 2004
813'.54—dc22

                          2003021621
British Library Cataloging-in-Publication Data available

To Olaf

October 17, 1984

At about five that afternoon, the East Science Facility sank into unnatural quiet. Most Municipal College students had already fled to buses and parking lots and the liveliness and warmth of home. Evening classes did not begin till six. On the first floor of the squat windowless building that looked like a warehouse, only two classes in English were winding down. Someone peeping through the glass window in the door of Room 101 could catch Lucille Streng at the blackboard, underlining topic sentences for the wakeful few in her remedial class.

Next door in Room 102, Igor Blavatsky sat on his desk in his green tweed suit, puffing a clandestine cigarette and dreaming of Odessa. Under the humming of the fluorescent light fixture and the hissing of the fitful streams of air that passed for ventilation in ESF, his freshman comp students bent their heads to ponder their essay question: Are Happy Families All Alike?

In Room 103, a disused classroom where normally no air blew, the English department subcommittee on the prelaw major had been in session since three o'clock. Deadlocked on a crucial vote to require *The House of the Seven Gables*, its members sat slumped in exhaustion. "I move to return to the Committee of the Whole," said the Chair in a voice clotted with fury. "All in favor?" Steve Speck fingered his five o'clock shadow. Five faint voices said, "Aye."

On the second floor of ESF—the biology labs—rats and guinea pigs scurried restlessly in their cages, awaiting dinner. A lone white-coated technician sat in a supply closet, meditatively smoking a joint.

On the top floor, the narrow corridors of ESF grew even narrower, linking twenty-two windowless faculty cubicles. By five o'clock the men and women of the English department had fled their cells, all but one devoted soul, as the faint clacking in the middle distance of a Royal manual typewriter testified, Cherry Binder working on a draft for *Feminist English Today*.

The maddeningly slow elevator—made for the handicapped—rose to the third floor. Elisabeth Hofrichter, maintenance person for ESF, slowly stepped out. Taking her time and muttering to herself, "God! My papers are in order. Always!" she unlocked the broom closet and pulled out the tall trash barrel on wheels. Jingling her keys back into her pants pocket, she pushed the barrel down the hall. Her barrel was fat, her back in its rough twill maintenance uniform extensive. No human could push past her. *"Alles in Ordnung."* She nodded her head.

Elisabeth unlocked the first faculty office, flipped the light switch, reached in—the cubicle could barely hold two chairs, a desk, file cabinet, and wastebasket—and emptied the trash into her barrel. "Papers in order, do they believe or not, *Gott* my witness." She pulled the door closed, and, taking two steps, unlocked the neighboring office door with the same key. "Papers," she said. She switched on the light and screamed.

On the floor of ESF 309, Lauren Goldberg lay, a pool of blood soaking the green industrial carpet.

In a little alcove of the faculty lunchroom under the plastic ficus sat two powerful members of the Personnel and Budget Committee, the departmental hiring and firing arm. While ordinary members of the English department were still scurrying over from ESF for lunch, Dickie Walter and Daphne Pryce-Jones, both released from their classroom responsibilities, were already on dessert.

"Natural causes," Dickie said, dipping his tea bag into the tepid water from the cafeteria urn. He loved to be first with information. "Lauren suffered an aneurysm. Then she fell and slit her scalp on the desk edge—bloody!

I had it from her brother-in-law who answered the tele-phone. Completely unexpected, unpredictable. Never had a sign before. Didn't she used to run a mile before break-fast and eat macrobiotic? Take step class? Work out with free weights? *Sunt lacrimae rerum.*" He turned to his card-board pie.

"I wonder if I can get her office," said Daphne in her clipped English accent. "It's highly desirable. Quiet, near the ladies'. Surprising she'd have a good spot like that."

Dickie looked startled. "Would you really want it, scene of a death and all?"

"Of course I do. If you worked next door to loud-mouth Lucille Streng, you'd take a bloodstain, too."

"Who'll get Lauren's line, do you think?"

Daphne chuckled. "I have a pretty good idea."

Nearby in a dim corner Cherry Binder was stuck with dim Mary Burnson, who taught Romantic Poetry. They'd both charged out the back door of ESF at the same moment and remained attached despite a long charade on Cherry's part of looking for a lost earring.

"Forty maids with forty mops can't get that blood-stain off the office rug," Cherry said. "The cleaning woman won't go near it. They're going to have to find an outside contractor."

Mary Burnson found Cherry Binder a cold fish. "I saw Lauren's coffee mug still on the shelf in the English office," she said, frowning and shaking her lank blonde hair. "Tragic, really. Only thirty-six years old, and on the verge of a full professorship. Heartbreaking. When I passed her classroom last night, her students were huddling around her desk and weeping all over the place."

"That's because she already gave the midterm."

In the center of the room at one of the tables for eight, three graduate assistants were wolfing down the daily special—chicken pie. The large round tables were supposed to encourage collegiality, but they rarely filled up. Although unimportant in the departmental scheme of things, grad students always knew the juiciest gossip.

"Awkward time to take over a class—around midterms," mused Harry Rhett, the oldest living graduate assistant, in a low southern voice. "And it's too late to use your own textbooks."

"But why did the police rope off the whole top floor of ESF?" Heidi Weismuller said, poking her piecrust with a fork tine. "I couldn't get up there to get my proficiency exams. Can't they recognize a natural death?"

"What is natural?" observed Betsy Fuller, who would have studied philosophy if only there were more jobs.

By this time, half past noon, the noise in the lunchroom was brutal. In that hubbub it was hard for the most accomplished eavesdropper to catch a word. Professors leaned forward hungrily across the Formica to catch the simple drift of their companions' speech. In the great goulash of conversation, no one could tell who was saying what.

"They were lovers. The husband knew since last semester. If only Lauren hadn't died of natural causes, he'd be number one suspect. The husband, I mean. George wouldn't hurt a flea." These remarks seemed to emanate from Sally Gonzalez of the French department.

"The English department has been having many disasters lately, have they not?" These words, or something like them, floated from the lips of Giuseppe Crostini, chairman of the comparative literature department, as he struggled with the gluey chicken-flecked filling. "Did you hear about their wrong estimates for preregistration? Shortsighted cheeseparing. No flair. Enrollment dropping. Far too little publicity."

At a drafty table near the door, Allen Swain dispensed his wisdom. "*You* could get that job, Steve, you're in Lauren's field, you've got the credentials. The trick is to nail down the job before they advertise. I'd say nail it down within three or four weeks."

"But how do I nail it down?" said Steve Speck. "I'm just a lecturer, not an assistant professor. I'm not even in the running."

"If you can't figure out how to get the job, you don't deserve it." Allen Swain laughed. "Come round to my office after my class and I'll plan your advancement. But remember, Steve, if you don't do exactly what I say, you might lose the job you have. And don't discuss this with anyone else."

The Chair of the English department wiped his chubby hands on his paper napkin and rose from his tabernacular table behind a pillar, a favorite hideout. "We'll have to let Lucille organize a memorial service. She likes that sort of thing. Keep her out of mischief. If we have it at night, we'll attract Lauren's students. Hold it, say, at six o'clock so we can get some day people, too. We'll get a date on the college calendar. Nail it down within three or four weeks."

"God, no, Ed," replied Alf Bjornsen, who taught Celtic studies. "Are you joking? I wouldn't go to my own mother's funeral after six P.M. on a weeknight. Why don't you put it on videotape and show it at the next department meeting?"

Professors Quinton Bloch (American lit) and Maurice el-Okdah (African-American studies) had little to say to each other but agreed to share the only remaining table in the lunchroom, a table for four at the heart of the noisy crowd.

"Lauren sat next to me at the last department meeting," said Maurice (Murray), shaking his distinguished head. "She was blooming, the picture of health."

"On the shelf?" said Quinton. "What did you say? Something about wealth?"

Brian McGlinchee, an untenured assistant professor, a large smooth young man with large smooth cheeks, approached their table, smiling broadly. "Gentleman, may I join you?"

"Did you hear about Lauren?" Murray asked, as Brian shoved out his chair.

"Mmm," Brian replied, discreetly moderating his smile. "It's always sad when a young person dies."

"Lauren was supposed to chair the symposia series next semester," Quinton said. "Horrible task. Now we'll have to search around for a replacement."

"I'm willing, really more than willing, *eager*," Brian said.

"Why did it have to happen to her?" said George Reilly to himself. He was sitting at the undesirable little table for two right near the cashier. People picking up coffee stirrers and sugar packets kept bumping into his chair. The last time he'd sat here, he and Lauren had quarreled. George's handsome face crumpled. "Why did I lose control of myself? Why did I say such nasty things? Lauren, forgive me."

Because George didn't have a class till two, he remained seated while all the other tables emptied, staring morosely at the exit. Then a cleaning person with a mop asked him to vacate, please.

1

W. C. Fields's alcoholic face leered out from Allen Swain's office. He wore a dented derby, puffed a cigar.

Steve had once been startled by this raffish note in the staid corridors of Temp 6, but as his treks to the English office became routine, he stopped noticing the leering image. Now he paused, face to face with Fields. The movie poster screened the Plexiglas panel which made each private office a public space.

"I wonder why other people haven't put up posters for privacy," Steve mused as he rapped on the ill-fitting steel-frame door. "Good idea."

"Come," Allen called.

Steve stuck his head in the door. "Busy?"

Allen, a smallish man with a delicate tanned face, was perched on his desktop busily stapling notices. "Come-ons for my next film class," he said. "Done in a jiffy!" He waved the photocopies.

Still on the threshold Steve recognized Marilyn Monroe's iconographic smile. He stepped inside and sat down in the plastic visitor's chair.

This wasn't Steve's first view of a Temp 6 office (he'd been hired in the Chair's double office at the end of the hall), but he was struck again by the wealth of spaciousness. Rundown and flimsy as Temp 6 was—set up as a temporary structure to house the rapidly growing English department about twenty-five years ago—it was Radio City compared with ESF.

Here was room to stand up and pace for three or four lengths while composing a comment on a student theme, ample space for a typing table, room even for a bookcase. A professor didn't have to worry about knees nuzzling a student's inadvertently during a conference. Best of all, a window—air, light, even a view (the blank siding of Temp 5 and a white drainspout).

"Look, let's not stay here," Allen said, putting down his papers and jerking his chin right and left at the brightly lit panel across from his office, Quinton's stout professorial figure within. He pointed to his ear and grimaced. He was always making boyish faces, and looked boyish from far away. Seen close up, his leathery skin was etched with fine wrinkles.

"Let's get something at Donuts R Us."

Allen led Steve off, slamming his door with a bang so that W. C. Fields shivered. As they walked down the dingy carpet to the exit, they saw Brian McGlinchee approaching.

Brian hailed them eagerly. "Yo, Steve," he said. "Are you headed to the office now?"

"No. Allen and I are going for coffee."

Brian regarded Allen intently. Two spots of high color burned his cheeks as if he were feverish, and his eyes moved restlessly behind his aviator frames. "I saw your piece in the last *International Film*. Very fine work. I really enjoyed it."

Allen bowed, smiling, without comment and, after a second or two, Brian, also smiling, passed by.

"Now there's someone you would do well to emulate," Allen murmured as they passed through the heavy glass door to the outside.

"McGlinchee? How so?"

"He's poised. He's friendly."

"He's not that friendly."

Despite their smiles, Steve's relations with Brian were on the cool side. When Steve had been assigned to McGlinchee's office two years ago, Brian was livid. No other full-time faculty member had to share an office; the space was barely big enough for one.

Because Steve taught at night, it was easy at first to keep out of Brian's way. They saw each other only at department meetings; the rest of the time they left civilized notes on the desk: "Do you know how to turn up thermostat?" "There isn't any." "Do you know where the stapler went?" "No idea."

But this semester, Brian had an evening class. Even though Steve avoided their office, conferring in the cafeteria, empty classrooms, or in the hall, whenever Brian glimpsed him, he'd ask, "Are you going to the office now?" Steve felt like sandbagging him.

Allen's silver Porsche was parked just outside Temp 6 right up against the chain link fence that separated the Municipal campus from surrounding garden apartments. The fading afternoon sun glinted on Allen's curling silvery hair as he unlocked his matching car door.

"How did you manage to get an office in Temp 6?" Steve asked in frank admiration, knocked out by the burgundy leather appointments of the car but too polite to ask the more impertinent "How did you get this great car?"

Allen chuckled and made as if to whisper in Steve's ear. "Disability," he hissed. "I told the secretary who made the mysterious office assignments—she was before your time, named so appropriately Sybil—that I had claustrophobia. Well, I did, actually, many years ago and it's always possible it might recur."

"So it wasn't a lie," Steve said simply.

"No, it wasn't a lie, but a resurrection of an old truth for strategic purposes."

Allen drove rapidly through the campus alleyways

to the main gate, then turned left on Lima Boulevard with a flourish. "So I'm over there with the bigwigs even though I'm a little wig, and it's wonderfully convenient. I hardly have to move a step. All the world comes to me. The associate chairman, the assistant chairman for composition, the assistant chairman for general studies, a few other indispensable functionaries, and me. In splendor. Dickie and Daphne have been gnashing their teeth over my office for years, but what can they do? They should have thought about their health earlier."

The corner doughnut shop at the traffic light was almost deserted at this time of day. Allen and Steve settled themselves in a red plastic booth, a cozier nook than the faculty lunchroom.

"Try the cream-filled chocolates, Steve. The praline is also yummy."

When Steve first met Allen on the Committee for the Prelaw Major, he'd been put off by the older man's extravagant poses. A casual dresser himself, he thought Allen's diminutive belted Norfolk jacket and suede Austrian woodsman's cap bizarre and believed the man was gay. Subsequent references to the ruinous costs of child support dimmed that idea.

A popular teacher with a flamboyant style, Allen filled huge lecture halls. Of course, as Dickie Walter put it—"Who couldn't attract students by showing movies? We'd all be overrun if we taught in the dark!"

The department considered film suspect, not rigorous enough, something like creative writing or women's studies—just a scam if you looked at it closely.

Allen didn't stay on campus much. He was an assiduous exchange professor with a knack for finding cushy spots at far-off universities. Although he was probably the most visible member of the department (with the possible exception of the African-American critic, Maurice el-Okdah, and the notorious Cherry Binder, who'd been arrested), he was not well liked.

"Now for the grand plan for your future," Allen said, with a sweeping gesture of his doughnut. He saw himself as urbane Addison DeWitt in his favorite movie, *All About Eve*. "If you're working as a lecturer at Muni College, you can be presumed to know nothing of advancement. There are only two ways to get ahead. One is by merit, but this is slow. Do you have time to wait till you've done the best work of your career? I think not.

"The other way is mediocrity. If you offend no one, you'll be offered tenure and live comfortably to a ripe old age. If you're brilliant and put the other department members in the shade, they'll cast you out. No one wants to be made to look ordinary. I understand you're working on a book?"

"Yes."

"What's it about?"

Steve put down his coffee mug and began to look

more lively. "You know the English poet Henry Martin? The one T. S. Eliot called the Country Toad? He's a fine poet, unjustly neglected. Well, Martin stopped writing altogether between 1914 and 1920. The fact is, no one even knows what he was doing during the First World War. He just disappeared from view. I propose to find out."

"Sounds more like an article than a book."

"Well, I'll also rehabilitate his reputation," Steve said without modesty.

"So, if your book finds a publisher and is well received, you'll be offered a professorship at some other college—that is, if there's no big recession. But it may not be in a city or on the East Coast. It might be in the country. You like the rural life?"

Steve shook his head no.

"You're used to the bright lights." Allen gestured to the narrow fluorescent fixture over the doughnut display case. "It's not certain you'll like living elsewhere and it's not certain you'll get a wonderful job, so your best bet is to dig in here."

"How did you get your job?"

"It wasn't due to brilliance on my part. Somebody died. In August luckily. They needed a replacement quick. Not many warm bodies in film around then.

"That was really long ago. My edges were rounder then. I had a charming wife at the time. Maybe she did me good. Who knows?" Allen looked through the dusty shopwindow at Lima Boulevard with a little melancholy twist of his lips.

"Now they're used to me, but they don't trust me. Too flashy. I'm an associate professor and I'll remain an associate professor, unless . . ."

"Unless . . . ?"

"As Nora said at the end of *A Doll's House*, if the most wonderful thing should happen. But there are no wonderful things in English departments! Why did you let them take advantage of you by hiring you as a mere lecturer? Weren't you warned?"

"No."

"You had no mentor?"

"No."

Allen clapped him on the arm, leaving a light dusting of sugar on Steve's green corduroy sleeve. "Well, you have one now. Your first mistake was to take this terrible job!"

"It didn't seem so terrible. The chairman said they wanted me, but they had no money. They only had one line—for a lecturer."

"Foolishness! Budget lines can be arranged, if necessary. If they really want you, they let someone else go, or pull strings to get a line from some other department. You might have a future here if you can grab Lauren's line, but you must follow the rules.

"The first rule you've already broken. Be visible! You allowed yourself to be given an evening schedule and if you're here at night you might as well be dead. First thing, ask for a day schedule for next semester."

"I like the night students," Steve protested. "Older students are more interesting." But Allen swept on.

"Rule two—be as agreeable as possible to as many as possible. But you sit through our committee without saying a word, and I never heard you speak in department meetings. You never even say 'aye.' How will Dickie and Daphne get to know and love you?"

Steve looked more and more downcast, but he kept silent. He knew he'd violated rule number one by trying hard to be invisible. Thinking mistakenly that he had a very good job, his strategy was to keep it by staying out of sight. As a lecturer he could teach for five years without any commitment on the department's part to keep him on for life. He'd served for two years lying low and minding his own business and could expect another undisturbed three years to work on Henry Martin. He was inclined to take his wonderful three years and let the future take care of itself.

As for ass licking, which Allen called being agreeable, he'd never done it in his life, not in grammar school, high school, or college and certainly not in graduate school. It was too late to start now. Allen's sudden interest in him was certainly weird. Had he done something to invite it? He brushed at his sugary sleeve.

"As it happens, Steve, I do have one ear on the P & B and I'll be glad to promote your cause. There may be some special service you can perform for the department. What appointed committees are you on besides prelaw?"

"Just the Library Committee."

"Library." Allen gave a groan. "That's sudden death. Buried alive. Any grants in the works?"

"No."

"Do you play tennis?"

"No."

"Any other sports?"

"Swim. A little."

"That's okay, but it's not very social. You won't influence anyone crawling along in the water. Your prospects don't look promising, but I'd say give it a whirl, anyway. You've nothing to lose except possibly your job."

"Is it really so dangerous?" Steve asked, laughing a bit. "Aren't you exaggerating?"

"I am not, dear boy." Allen tilted his head to one side in his leprechaun pose from *Finian's Rainbow*. "I don't know how you ever got your Ph.D. You must lead the charmed life of the innocent. Tell me, you don't drink or take drugs or do anything that would be embarrassing? You don't molest students?"

Steve shook his head.

Allen chuckled. "You're awfully quiet for an English teacher."

Steve didn't reply.

The next day, Steve forgot about his small pile of bills and his huge stack of papers to grade. Feeling cheerful, he went for a swim at the West Side Y. Then he took a long hot bath while reading *Traveler* and prepared himself to meet his girlfriend.

Despite recent success with women, Steve wasn't a real ladies' man. By the time of his high school graduation he'd never gone on a single date or kissed a girl. He'd spent his high school days immersed in his schoolwork, his computer, and his violin.

His dating problems were solved in college when women began asking him out. They were remarkably eager and patient. When he'd neglect to call them because he had a long paper to write or because he'd been swallowed up by a new computer chess opponent, they telephoned him. If he forgot to make advance arrangements for a dinner or a weekend, they quickly stepped in to do all the tiresome paperwork. What an amazing sex, he always thought at the start of a romance. His initial sex partner was his freshman French teacher at Swarthmore, whose special tutoring woke him up from his dream and left him with a lifelong weakness for petite dark girls with barely defined moustaches.

"You're gentle and sensitive, not exploitive like most men," girls always said to Steve at the beginning. "Cold! Weak!" they'd end up exclaiming. "Can't you even remember my birthday?"

Aimee continued the tradition, picking him up at a party at his former violin teacher's house after he gave her an admiring stare. Within five minutes she invited him to her favorite midtown club. He didn't dance. She brought him to her parents' Fifth Avenue apartment and seduced him in record time on her own bed to her own carefully chosen flamenco tape, a solea of missed connections and unfulfilled desires. "Don't mind if I do" was Steve's attitude on these occasions, though he'd pulled himself together to the extent of carrying condoms.

Everything about Steve was well shaped—long legs, slim torso, a large noble head with thick dark hair and large blue eyes fringed with long black lashes. He could sometimes be witty, especially when he'd had a few drinks, though he had no control over his witticisms and later regretted his babbling. Most of the time he was silent, and this silence and his noble head drove girls to fall speedily in love with him.

This evening Aimee was scheduled to arrive at Steve's place, and if the previous weekends were any precedent, they weren't likely to stir outside except possibly to the Chinese restaurant on the corner. Aimee was lying low from her parents, who didn't know that their daughter had left Bennington and returned to Manhattan for the weekend. How Aimee managed to keep up her grades while traveling back and forth from Vermont by bus nearly every weekend, Steve couldn't imagine. She never brought schoolwork with her, and once, when Steve questioned her about her courses, she gave him a slow enigmatic smile and said between her teeth, "Let's say I'm passing without distinction."

Steve felt odd being the lover of a college girl. If Aimee were a student in one of his own classes at Muni, he might get into trouble for fraternizing. He realized that she saw him as a romantic figure—older man, college professor.

Aimee also thought Steve's apartment glamorous because of its tinge of squalor. After a long search, he'd managed to find a cheap place in the last old law tenement on Columbus Avenue, up a narrow dank-smelling staircase to a railroad flat over a bar. "Oh, this is wonderful!" Aimee cried the first night she arrived and saw the reflection of the red neon sign flashing COLLINS BAR in the windows. She pronounced the small old-fashioned bathroom with claw-legged tub "too cool." She left two peacock feathers in a mayonnaise jar on the top of the commode to signify her pleasure.

Aimee wasn't a stereotypical twenty-year-old. She was a lapsed violin player, a lapsed creative writer, a lapsed sculptor, woodworker, silversmith. Right now her medium was dried flowers. All her little idiosyncrasies delighted Steve—her long Pre-Raphaelite hair, her purple-and-rose-dyed wardrobe, her allergy to base metals, her scent of jasmine and attar of roses. Her bedroom with its willow furniture, low to the ground, was the lair of a wild creature.

Days were getting shorter and the wind howled in the courtyard outside the kitchen window as Steve stood at the range preparing butterscotch pudding for their evening treat. As soon as Aimee rang from the musty vestibule, he'd dash downstairs to fetch up her heavy backpack, and, after a few moments of hugs and gossip, they'd collapse on the Salvation Army bedstead in the front room. An expensively dressed tigress, Steve would say as he struggled with her tiger-striped panty hose to expose her tanned rear. She scorned underpants. She scorned bras. Her body was superb. All this flashed through his mind and he hadn't a care for his future tenure as he patiently stirred the butterscotch powder around in the milk-filled saucepan.

But when Aimee arrived in the actual flesh, nothing happened as planned. The buzzer rasped. Steve dashed down. Aimee stood without any smiles. She stamped up the stairs as if angry with each tread. She made no exclamations of delight over the gallon of cider he'd lugged all the way home from the Farmer's Market and kept sitting with a loose cap on the kitchen sill. She ignored the new spray of bittersweet on the brown mantel. She produced no present for him this week, no pot of honey or volume of Rilke's poems.

"What's the matter, sweetie? What happened?"

"I lost my favorite scarf in the taxi."

"Too bad. Maybe you can call the taxi company. Do you remember the name of the driver?"

"Are you joking?"

Aimee sulked about her loss for a while as if it were Steve's fault. Then she said, "I'm just grumpy because I have my period."

Why did she travel all the way here? This crude thought flashed through Steve's mind before he could censor it.

Then she cried and sat on his lap and revealed that she was flunking all her courses except art. The only solution was to leave Bennington and come and live with him, or else go study drama in London, but she'd have to fix that up with her parents; it would take a while.

In panic Steve thought at once, "Study drama in London." He didn't say a word, but held Aimee on his lap and ran his hand up and down her smooth stockinged leg in a soothing fatherly stroke. At least it was fatherly at first, but the embrace soon grew erotic. "I'll unplug for you," Aimee said finally and went off cheerfully to the bathroom. That was a first for Steve.

Steve's huge stack of freshman papers had shrunk but not enough. It was twenty minutes before class, and six five-hundred-word themes remained in an untidy stack on his desk. Because of budget cuts, his office was crypt cold, so Steve sat swaddled in an old Shetland sweater and a woolly scarf, his red marking pencil in his hand, his eyes racing across the page.

> In my opinion I thought the play was good, but there were some improvements necessary. At first, I wasn't very impressed with the play because I thought it wasn't interesting. The reason why I thought it wasn't interesting was because the dialogue was too long. Another reason was because the actors and actresses didn't do their best acting. A third reason was the language wasn't to clear. I couldn't understand some of the speaking.

Steve wrote REPETITIOUS in his big scrawling hand. Then he wrote WHY? EXPLAIN. He thought for a while and wrote WORDY/AWK. Then he gave up; he pushed aside his papers and unwrapped a small brown paper bag containing hummus and red peppers on whole wheat pita, a tasty but skimpy dinner. With any luck the freshmen would forget to ask for their essays.

Ever since Allen's lecture in the doughnut shop, Steve had been thinking about money. He'd been slowly sliding into debt since he began working at Muni and discovered that teaching English was a delightful enterprise that left lots of time for pleasure and nothing much to spend on its pursuit. His graduate tuition at Columbia had eaten up everything his father had left him. His mother's remarriage and move to California had pretty much cut off that rich source of cash gifts. Now his toaster oven was dead, his VCR would play but not record, his winter parka was slowly leaking goosedown, and his next paycheck a whole month away.

If he were an assistant professor, he could begin the exciting part of his research right away. Instead of riding the squalid E train out to Muni campus for summer school and spending the remains of the steaming day crouched in library stacks over yellowing magazines, he could be on British Airways, hot on Henry Martin's trail. The thought was exhilarating. On June 1 he could be driving on the wrong side of the road, drinking cider in a pub. Or drudging in libraries over yellowing magazines, but at least they would be English libraries.

With his forefinger Steve pursued the little bits of parsley that had fallen out of his pita onto the desk and munched them meditatively. Allen Swain was certainly the serpent in the garden of his fantasy life. Steve balled up the waxed paper in the brown paper bag and tossed it into the wastepaper basket in the kneehole of his desk. He must be neat because of Brian, whom he'd observed carefully wiping the desk with a paper towel before each use. The leather-trimmed blotter, the embossed appointment pad, and the celadon mug full of sharply pointed number two pencils all belonged to Brian. So did the color photo in the silver frame, which showed a beaming Brian, his buxom blonde wife, and two alarmingly small children posed proudly in front of a gleaming Honda.

As Steve bent over the battered metal waste can, his eye was caught by a pattern of purple ink on pale pink stationery at the bottom. Not your ordinary academic announcement. He bent forward to squint at the note, his head almost under the desk. A seductive scent of lilacs and lilies rose to his nostrils. He quickly plucked the letter out of the basket and began smiling. Addressed to Brian, it read as follows:

Dear Prof. McGlinchee:

Here is my Wife of Bath essay for you to excoriate. In case you want to reach me before our next class, here is my work and my home telephone number. English 79 is giving me nightmares. Could we spend a few minutes talking about it next Thursday? I need lots of moral support, which only you can provide. Thanks.

Cynthia Lovitt

"Oh, boy," Steve said out loud, his smile turning to a smirk. Some student was after Brian! How wonderful. He gave the pink notepaper a deep sniff, then, tickled by this exotic note, popped the interesting missive into his briefcase.

Steve looked around to see if Brian's briefcase was behind the coatrack. It was. Though Brian didn't teach tonight, he'd recently taken to turning up at odd hours. Steve made it a point of honor to leap up at a moment's notice and vacate. Brian seemed harassed lately; he kept losing his office key and misplacing books. Before class he opened and reclosed drawers, shuffling through many folders, muttering under his breath. Up for tenure soon, Brian was probably working too hard.

Some senior professors never entered their offices; from the corridor Steve could hear their telephones ringing plaintively and see bored students squatting on the green industrial carpet outside their doors. Untenured, Brian omitted nothing. No paper remained ungraded, no mimeographed form—no matter how lowly—remained unfilled out. No absences, no latenesses, no challenges by disappointed students, no complaints of any kind. No wonder he was acting rattled.

Steve heard thumping outside and the clinking of keys in the lock, but instead of Brian, the cleaning woman flung open the door.

"Papers?"

"Good evening. I'm afraid the can's empty tonight. Not too much activity here, sorry to say."

The cleaner ducked her head and made as if to flee, but Steve had a sudden thought and arrested her in mid-flight. She was sort of birdlike for a heavy woman.

"I'm sorry. I'm sorry. I forgot about my sandwich."
As he gabbled, Steve bent forward to retrieve the brown
paper bag. The cleaning woman also bent forward and
their heads clinked together with a crack.

The cleaner shrieked and shuttled her head. "*Gott in
Himmel*, Mister! Stars and planets!"

Scared, Steve sprang out of his office chair and
grabbed her twilled shoulder. "Here, sit down. I didn't
mean to hurt you." He plunked her into his chair. "It was
just an accident. Shall I get you some wet paper towels?"

"No one knows how I suffer," the woman said, resting her thick forearms on his desk and groaning. "All
things together . . . too much, how must I bear this?"

Steve sat down in the student's chair beside the desk
and tried to soothe her. "I know your job must be hard.
I've watched you going around here every night. I know
how hard you work. Why, this floor is immaculate. It's
the cleanest building on the campus. You do a great job!"

The woman turned to look at him with a mild look
of surprise. "I've seen you too, young gentleman. Outside
when I clean *Toiletten*."

"What's your name?"

"Elisabeth Hofrichter. Afraid to be fired any
moment. No money! Moneyless!"

"I'm Steve Speck. No money either! I can be fired,
too. I have a contract to the end of the year but that's it."

Elisabeth shook her head. "*Also*, we're two birds

alike." She rose heavily to her feet. "I will look out, every-thing in order to make. *Auf Wiedersehen*, Doktor Speck."

She made a dignified exit, not forgetting the brown paper bag. Steve, exhausted, sank back into his chair.

Within two minutes, Steve heard the keys clinking again and Brian came bustling into the room, carrying two Bloomingdale's bags. Steve was too demoralized to spring up.

"No, don't get up." Brian waved at Steve, his ruddy close-shaven face oddly cheerful. With demonic energy he opened a desk drawer on his side and began stuffing folders into the bags. "The office is now yours for a while, Steve. I'm moving over to Temp 6 as of today. I'm new head of programs."

"No kidding." Steve smiled broadly.

"Alf Bjornsen was attacked in Central Park, got a stab wound in the gut. He'll be on disability at least till June, maybe longer."

"Where in Central Park? What happened?"

"Don't know. I'm sort of weak in the service to the department area so this move is a godsend. But it's no pic-nic, making up people's programs, a good way to make every goddamn person in the department mad at you."

"But some people must be very happy."

"I don't play that way, Steve," Brian said, glaring. "Evenhandedness is my motto." He reached over Steve's shoulder, picked up the color photo of his family, and dumped it in the shopping bag.

Any point in asking Brian for a daytime schedule for next semester? Steve thought gloomily. Actually my program can't get much worse. He remembered his father's favorite proverb—"You can't fall out of bed when you're sleeping on the floor." His father, a law graduate of the late thirties, had settled for a dull job in the floor tile business.

Brian squeezed past Steve to the filing cabinet and began culling more files. "You can have the stapler, the paper clips, and all the college stationery. I'll use Bjornsen's." He crumpled up a sheet of paper and angled around Steve to toss it in the can. "Oh, that reminds me. I left an important telephone number in the garbage this morning." He made as if to shoulder Steve aside.

"Sorry," Steve replied in a strangled voice. He couldn't very well reach inside his briefcase to produce the note. "The cleaning woman came by already. The can is empty."

"Oh," said Brian. His voice was steely. "My mistake."

Cherry Binder sometimes gave Steve a ride home. She lived on West 96th Street, and dropped him off on Central Park West before turning uptown.

Steve didn't enjoy those rides because Cherry was a world-class terrible driver. Blithely cutting off other cars at will, she never glanced in her rearview mirror. In the midst of an intense little lecture on Virginia Woolf she darted without looking into the next lane. Last spring,

when she was pregnant, she caressed her belly negligently with one hand while she cut right on Lima Boulevard.

Still, after spending a full day and an evening on
campus, Steve sometimes felt he'd rather die in a flaming
crash than ride the subway to Manhattan, so he'd pop
into Cherry's classroom on the ground floor near the exit
and ask for a lift after class. She never refused him,
though once or twice she'd absentmindedly left without
him.

Tonight, after two grueling composition classes, five
sluggish student conferences, and two unsettling encoun-
ters with Elisabeth Hofrichter and Brian McGlinchee,
Steve felt wiped out. He decided to go downstairs to Cherry's classroom and ask for a lift. As he approached, Steve
spotted Cherry charging out with her infant bundled in
her arms.

Even before her pregnancy Cherry had cut a
remarkable figure. With her strong flawless teeth, her
handsome profile on a pillarlike neck, her odd costumes
of leggings, smocks, and boots, and her beret perched on
her head like a sign of instability, Cherry could never be
overlooked in a crowd.

"Here, Steve, hold Morley for me while I put on my
hat," Cherry said, juggling her briefcase, beret, and baby.
"The stupid baby-sitter didn't show up, so I had to bring
Morley to class." Cherry shook out her abundant hair and
reached for her child. "Why is it so dark in the corridor?"

"They unscrewed every other lightbulb. Budget reasons. Did the class go all right?"

"Morley was marvelous. He slept through the entire lecture, but it was hard to focus everyone's attention. I must find a reliable baby-sitter. When I'm teaching, I have to forget I have a baby."

Steve had always wondered about Cherry's domestic arrangements, but he didn't like to ask. He knew that Cherry's husband was living in Dallas because he couldn't get a teaching job in New York. He'd been there for five years! Now that Morley had arrived, the arrangement sounded stressful, at least for Cherry.

"What I really need is a student who'll baby-sit for me here on campus. That would be convenient and save me lots of dough."

Despite her sometimes peremptory behavior, Steve had a soft spot for Cherry. Unlike the other professors, she always said hello when they passed in the corridors. On the quad she'd wheel around and salute him; sometimes she even remembered to ask after Henry Martin.

Tonight the car trip to Manhattan was more harrowing than usual. Morley lay in an unsafe heap on the front seat beside Cherry. Wrapped up in his cotton blanket, he was just the right size to fit into Steve's battered briefcase. Now Morley's raw salmon-colored face held an inward meditative look as if he were digesting the literary thoughts of the evening.

"Why don't I hold him?"

"Sure—good idea."

As usual Cherry barreled along highway and street at top speed talking a mile a minute about her proposed new course, Narrative Lies: Constructions of Race, Class and Gender. "But I don't think the department will go for it. They're not big on personal identity and selfhood."

"Allen Swain says I have a chance to get Lauren's line," Steve confided in a pause for change at the mid-town tunnel.

"No doubt at all, they'll replace Lauren with a man," Cherry said darkly.

"But do you think *I* have a chance to be the man?" Steve persisted.

"Who knows? They think in such strange ways."

In no time at all they jerked to a stop on Central Park West. Steve kissed Morley's soft drooly chin and set him back down on the seat, then paused with his hand on the door handle.

"Are you sure you'll be okay? I can see you home and then take the bus back downtown."

Cherry gave him a withering look. "Twenty blocks—big deal!" she said. "I'll buy a car seat tomorrow. Just slam the door and get out of here!"

Steve hurried along the cold dark street toward Columbus Avenue, sighing with relief when he finally glimpsed his shabby, paint-chipped door. No one would believe how tired he was. He could hardly haul himself up the stairs.

Aimee was sitting on his Salvation Army sofa in the living room, painting her toenails. "You look dead," she said, smiling.

"I feel dead." He hoisted his briefcase. "Here we have sixty more freshman papers to read, and I never finished the last set."

"You spend too much time sitting. That's why you're tired."

"Is there anything to eat?"

"Beer, pretzels, goat cheese salad, strudel."

He wanted to give Aimee a hug but was afraid he would upset her tiny bottle, which said CELLINI GOLD.

"Let's take the day off tomorrow and go for a walk at Battery Park City. And maybe the movies in the evening?"

"No, I have a committee meeting in the morning, and then there's the freshmen. I wouldn't begrudge them the time if I really thought I was helping them . . ."

"Of course you're helping them. You're their role model for cleverness."

"You're the only one left who thinks I'm clever. I used to be clever before I started teaching at Muni."

"You still are, baby. You're just losing your self-esteem."

"If I could just get Lauren's line . . ."

Aimee rolled her eyes. "A line. It sounds like a fishing line."

"We can't go to the movies tomorrow night. I have to stay for Lauren's memorial service. Pay my respects. Show my departmental spirit."

"There's something bizarre about that English department, if you ask me. Will they have an open coffin?"

Scandalized, Steve moved away from the sofa and threw himself down on the rug beside his Chess Strategist. "Lauren has been dead for more than a month," he said. "And I haven't done a thing about that line."

2

The ground floor of the student union always reminded Steve of the Great Temple of Karnak. The building was huge, and it seemed to go on and on, one bare lofty concrete pillar followed by another bare lofty concrete pillar, not such a cozy space for students to hang out.

From all over the campus a thin stream of mourners was flowing along the battered concrete walkways towards the student union to attend Lauren Goldberg's memorial service. The stream coagulated in the lobby of the union, waiting to fill up the elevator. When the doors opened, the crowd surged in with the brisk brutality of New Yorkers. Among the students, Steve spotted a faculty face or two he recognized from department meetings, but no one he knew well enough to greet.

Just before the elevator doors closed, a slight man elbowed in, and Steve recognized Allen, holding a steaming plastic container of tea or coffee against his chest. Steve felt a twinge of guilt at seeing Allen's clever tanned face, now breaking into a smile. Still, he hadn't entered into any kind of compact, no matter what Allen thought. It wasn't a sin to want a better job. It wasn't a sin to do little about it.

When the elevator disgorged on the fourth floor, seat of the Milliken Memorial Chapel, the two men met with relief in the hallway and let the crowd push past.

"I have to sit near the door," Allen said. "I'm only making a pro forma appearance. An appointment on the Lower East Side in forty minutes—I'm leaving shortly."

"Wish I could go with you. I've been here since nine this morning." Steve's voice took a peevish note. "Thanks so much for getting me on the Prizes Committee. Did you know they met at the crack of dawn?"

"Best I could do, old chap. Could have been worse. Could have been evaluations or appeals. Long hours at registration, or confrontations and tears." He lowered his voice. "I spoke to my informant about the budget cuts. The news is bad but not quite as bad as it seems."

The fourth floor corridor formed a circle. As the two men sauntered along the worn blue carpet, they peered through the glass porthole in each closed door, looking for the chapel. These portholes compensated for the absence of windows in the student union, windowlessness being a prominent feature of all recent construction on Muni campus.

While they peered, the crowd they'd belonged to so

briefly disappeared, and they fetched up in front of the elevators again.

"Luckily, it's not a total job freeze, just severe budgetary cuts. That means anyone with a yearly contract can be eliminated, but, thank God, we can replace our tenured faculty, those who leave or die."

"Those who leave or die . . . but there aren't many of those, are there?"

"Afraid not."

In a moment a second crowd disgorged and Allen and Steve tailed it more diligently. Because Steve taught mostly incoming freshmen, he didn't recognize any of the solemn student faces.

"Also, they're raising tuition. Second time in two years."

No wonder the students looked solemn.

This time around, one anonymous door stood open. Allen and Steve peered into a small semicircular auditorium with a podium, a wall hung with a tapestry (figure of white dove against navy blue ground), bare wooden pews with medieval-looking ladder backs. All the seats near the door were full.

"Damn," Allen whispered. "I'll have to crawl over everyone. Maybe I'll just leave now."

"Plenty of seats up front," a loud voice announced. A horse of a woman with buck teeth and frizzy hair came striding up the aisle to meet them. Lucille Streng, coordinator of the event. *"Hullo, Allen, nice to see you here,"* Lucille said in a surprised voice, as if spotting the Antichrist at early morning Mass. She glared at Allen's coffee cup and he meekly dumped it into the trash receptacle just inside the door. She nodded at Steve, her surgical-steel double-hoop earrings clinking against each other as she led the men to the very first row, obviously reserved for faculty.

The associate chair, Quinton Bloch, sat at the far end of the row staring at his fleshy fingertips and pulling at his bushy black walrus moustache. At their end, three seats in, George Reilly sat muttering over a black-leather gilt-edged book, his handsome face clenched in concentration. Further along Cherry Binder was in animated conversation with Brian McGlinchee, while on the other side Mary Burnson eagerly drank in their words. As Allen and Steve seated themselves, the sound of a keyboard imitating an organ came from some unknown nook. Steve recognized all-purpose Bach.

By six o'clock every bench in the chapel was packed tight. Lucille glanced at her watch a few times, then strode to the podium.

"Welcome, welcome, everyone. We've come to pay our respects to Lauren Goldberg. We all knew her. I've asked a few people I thought best exemplified her passion for teaching and her special light to speak tonight. First, though, the Twenty-third Psalm."

She gave it an upbeat reading, falling heavily on the words "pasture," "table," and "cup," and miming a staff in the air.

Everyone in the Department of English complained about Lucille Streng, her pushiness, her blasting laugh, her dimwitted mimeographed notices. Yet somehow Lucille served on every committee, chaired every function, and could not be suppressed. Her pushiness had a life of its own. Those unfortunate enough to fall into the quicksand of her presence struggled at first, but soon sank.

"Let me say a few words about Lauren before introducing the others, starting with a little anecdote I thought very revealing." Lucille gave a pleased anticipatory yip, meaning, You'll love this.

"Lauren was a terrific worker. She took on a lot of responsibility. She was busy but very well organized. When I served with her once on the University Task Force for Pluralism and Diversity, I was amazed at how quickly she completed her paperwork. How do you do it, I asked.

"Of course, she didn't have any children, which makes it hard on some of us women professors. But the work she did was truly amazing."

Lucille walked round to the front of the lectern, bent her knee and leaned her buttock against the mahogany. "I'll share with you what she told me, and you may want to use it in your own lives."

Allen nudged Steve sharply with his elbow. "Rather kill myself," he whispered.

"Lauren told me, 'I avoid clutter in everything I do, and I set limits. Whenever I buy a new dress or a skirt, before I hang it in my closet, I give or throw away another dress or skirt. I have many books in my library. Whenever I buy a new book I remove an unwanted volume from the shelves.'"

Lucille stopped and let the impact of her words sink in. "An unwanted volume from the shelves," she intoned. "Listen to her words, 'I set limits.' Think about them. Ask yourself . . ." Lucille paused and stared out at her audience. Steve shrank in his seat, hoping Lucille wouldn't call on him. "Would *you* have the courage to do the same?

"We will now have five minutes of silent meditation, then a brief selection by the Ars Longa Trio, Schubert's Trio no. 3. Unfortunately, the chair of the English department wasn't feeling well today and was forced to go home early, but we will hear a few words about Lauren Goldberg's scholarly accomplishments from the associate chair, and then a few more words from several of Lauren's students. But first, your silence!"

Lucille marched away from the podium and sat down next to Quinton Bloch with her head bowed. The long silence began. Instantly Steve's mind began to wander. Since grade school he'd been lousy at meditating. He could hear George Reilly still muttering on one side of him, and Allen's stertorous breathing on the other side. The fellow really was asthmatic.

Whom did Lauren give the skirt or dress to? Steve wondered. Did she have a regular recipient? Did she advertise? Did she manage to get her old goods out of the house on the same day the new ones arrived, or did they languish in cardboard boxes for a few days in the basement? Wasn't it about time for Allen to stand up and tiptoe away? Or did he think it wiser to wait to hear Quinton?

The meditation was definitely over because rustling broke out all over the audience in little shuffles and ripples. Allen shifted his flanks but did not stand. The Ars Longa Trio, flute, violin, and cello, three Asian girls dressed in tasteful black jumpers, scurried around the podium, setting up their music stands and whispering to each other. Just then George Reilly, still muttering to himself, stood up abruptly, threw off his tweed jacket and began bumping past Steve's knees towards the aisle. In baggy unspeakable trousers, he stumped to the lectern looking very pale, his longish untidy hair falling in clumps over his perspiring forehead.

Lucille was angry. "Here," she said. "What's he doing? He's not on the agenda. Here," she said with a snort. "George, you're not on the program."

George paid no attention. He gripped the lectern and with a strong visionary gleam stared out at the audience, who stared back transfixed. George was a very attractive man, "black Irish," with pale skin, black hair, green eyes. Tonight his skin had a greenish cast. Big globules of sweat stood out on his forehead.

"I'm here to pay tribute to my beloved, who was not appreciated while she was alive . . ." George passed his hand across his eyes, as if wiping away confusing thoughts. "It's hard to believe such perfection is gone. She was a rare human being, clever, kindhearted, a tiger in bed."

With scared faces the student musicians were backing away from George, holding on to their instruments and trying to disappear into the tapestry under the claws of the dove.

"Lauren was everything to me, all beauty and happiness. Her thighs were warm. The skin of her belly was downy and delectable."

Here Lucille put her head in her hands and rocked her stout body forward. Against their wills, a few mourners began turning their heads to their neighbors and smiling, or looking around to see if Lauren's husband was in the crowd.

"I never thanked her for my pleasure. I criticized her. I kept her waiting for a message. I forced her to call me at odd hours, all useless sadism." George stopped and gazed downward in despair. With a quick thrust of his right hand, he grabbed at the front of his wilted blue shirt and keened. Nothing happened for a moment. Then George jerked harder with both hands and popped off three shirt buttons, exposing his lean, marble-white chest bifurcated by a line of soft black down.

With a shriek the girl with the flute ran down the side aisle and out the door. The rest of the audience sat transfixed. "My God!" George wailed. "What's the use of being alive at all?"

While George was unbuckling his belt and unzipping his fly, Quinton Bloch, who had been a halfback in college, strode across the aisle and interposed his burly body between George and the audience. He was tall enough to reach the top of the lectern without ascending the step. "Hey, George, that's enough," he barked. "You've said enough. Get off the podium!" He fluttered his hands as if scattering chickens, and, to everyone's astonishment and disappointment, George meekly rezipped and rebuckled and placed his hand across his gaping shirtfront. He then moved off to the exit as if pledging allegiance to the flag. He looked backward with a sharp tilt of his head, as if he saw Lauren's angelic form in the bright top hat lighting in the ceiling.

"He's flipped," Steve said to Allen. "There goes his contract for next year."

"He has tenure. Nothing will happen. A semester off at full pay, some graduate assistant's big bonanza."

•

"Look, you'd better handle it," the Chair told Quinton Bloch. "I wasn't there, and I've heard conflicting reports. Maybe he was drunk."

"He wasn't drunk. In a mystical rapture, was more like it. He was rending his clothes and talking about her breasts and belly. Unstrung, totally. A loose cannon."

"Luckily no one from the *Weekly Munivox* was there. I checked. Their reporter got the day wrong. And not many from the department, mostly junior people. That's lucky, too. But Dean Cranbog was there, did you know that? Standing in the back. He was the first to call me.

"Dickie Walter had the flu, so he missed it and is sick with disappointment. Lucille is frothing at the mouth and wants George fired immediately. Daphne didn't bother to go and doesn't want to be bothered. So that leaves you, Quint."

"Me?"

"Should he be allowed to teach if he's acting erratically? Investigate. Is he dangerous? If so, check with the president's office. Most important, write a report so we have something on paper. I delegate all responsibility to *you*."

"Thanks a lot, Ed. What if he *is* dangerous? Why should it be my responsibility?

"You'll be chair after me and you ought to have some experience in dealing with potentially explosive situations. I'll write you a special commendation for your file, and the department will owe you a favor. Hmm . . . what's his schedule for today?" The Chair's plump fingers shuffled through the photocopied program cards in the gray metal box on his desk.

"Yes, due in ten minutes in ESF 102. Go over and catch him."

"What about my own class?"

"They'll wait for you, Quinton. I'll have Gloria run over with a message."

After Quinton left, the Chair summoned Ramona. "Under no circumstances do I ever want George Reilly in my private office. Tell him I'm busy and refer him *directly* to Professor Bloch.

"Now, I'm going to review the spring staffing needs, complicated work. I don't want to be disturbed." He closed the door and turned the key.

Breathing a bit heavily, the Chair hurried to his desk and removed his Blue Flower Farm catalog from the middle drawer. A flower bed near his deck was crying out for some hemerocallis. He'd combine lilies and daylilies in a manner not seen before in East Hampton.

Can I put Bright Banner next to Prairie Sunset? he mused, trying to summon up his complicated garden schema without his notes, which he'd absentmindedly left on top of the CD player at home. Bright Banner, red and golden bronze, blooming from July to September. Wouldn't that clash with oxblood Summer Interlude, a

July–August bloomer? What exactly was oxblood, a color like shoes?

Out front Ramona's phone rang urgently eight or nine times. "Where's Ramona?" He heard Lucille Streng's strident voice right outside his door. "I need some envelopes. She's got them locked up like Fort Knox. Where the hell is she?"

With piercing gaze the Chair studied the color photos of the brilliant lilies, retracted petals, prominent sex organs. He felt a bit anxious since his fall order hadn't arrived yet. He'd heard the demand was fierce, that some ruthless gardeners were even reselling bulbs.

Instead of Summer Interlude, how about Small Ways, only twenty inches, a pale lemon yellow? And for that little triangle at the end of the bike rack, a luscious mound of Stargazer, ringed perhaps by Raspberry Fizz? But when did Raspberry Fizz bloom? Would that site catch the noonday sun?

Outside the phone began ringing again even more urgently. I must be more methodical, he said to himself, making a note on an index card, and keep meticulous charts.

At that moment in ESF 101, Mary Burnson poked her head out the door, hoping to exchange a few words with George before Wordsworth, Shelley, and Keats began. Perhaps she'd invite him to lunch. Her pale cheeks had an unaccustomed flush of excitement as she looked first this way, then that way, down the dim corridor. Mary usually resembled a stately golden Afghan, but today she looked more like a terrier after a rat.

Her eagerness to catch George wasn't nosiness, she told herself. She knew she had a way of calming poor afflicted souls, of relieving them of pain simply by throwing herself open to their concerns. I was touched by the sincerity of your feelings for Lauren, she planned to say. I admire the way you defied convention to express your love.

Both Mary and George had been hired by the department on the same day eight years ago. Neither one had been promoted, which made a weakish bond between them. Mary, anxious to be of service to just about anybody, and George, always eager for a good time, had little else in common except for their pale white skins.

For years George enjoyed the role of departmental playboy. His colleagues loved to cluck over his passion for tennis and good-looking women and his feckless indifference to scholarly publication, but at the same time they liked George. He brightened the day with his high spirits, his willingness to linger in a stairwell or vestibule and clown and tell bad jokes. (George's imitation of a Nazi officer interrogating St. Bernadette of Lourdes was a highlight of his repertory. Mary always thought his humor in very poor taste.) But lately George had been much more subdued. Probably Lauren's calming influence.

Mary left her room and peeped into George's classroom next door, where three young women lounged at the back of the room under the coat hooks. One was glumly reading *The Village Voice*, another was glumly eating taco chips, and the third sat crumpled in her chair with her head on the armrest, her long red hair dangling down as if she'd been guillotined. A muscular young hood in torn jeans sat on the radiator eating a Mr. Goodbar. Not a likely crew for an advanced-level course with God knows how many prerequisites. Post-Thanksgiving doldrums, probably, or perhaps George had been too demoralized by grief to pay much attention to Beckett, Pinter, and the Postmodern Dilemma.

Suddenly Mary heard Quinton Bloch's bellowing voice in the corridor. "Have you seen Professor Reilly?"

She peeped outside to see Quinton interrogating Captain Jack, the elderly security guard, who usually spent his tour of duty resting on the bench in the vestibule of ESF, his rheumy eyes fixed on the revolving door.

"Nope, ain't seen him. Ain't been looking for him, neither."

Oh, no, they're after him, she thought in alarm. Persecuting the poor unfortunate fellow. She stepped into the corridor.

"Hullo, Mary," Quinton said without enthusiasm. "Think George will be in class today?"

"I imagine so. Why do you want him?"

"Just a little chat about last night's performance."

Captain Jack looked interested. "In trouble, eh?"

Quinton attempted to avoid Captain Jack's interest by turning to one side, but Captain Jack shuffled around into his line of vision.

"I heard all about it. Bare-assed at the funeral. Lots of sex remarks."

"Shouldn't you be at your post?"

"Kind of embarrassing. Wish I'd been there." The old man chuckled as he wandered back to the lobby.

"I'll go upstairs and look in his office. If he shows, tell him I'm looking for him. I'm due in Transcendentalism in two minutes. I can't hang around here."

No sooner had Quinton headed for the stairs than George appeared from the opposite direction. He looked much as usual, even a little better than usual. His moleskin trousers were crumpled and discolored, as if he'd been gardening, but he was wearing a clean maroon corduroy shirt with a matching knapsack slung over his shoulder, and his stride had an energetic lift. "Hello, Mary."

Mary blocked his path as quickly as she could. "I thought you might want to lunch with me later. I'm eager to talk to you."

"Good of you," he replied gently, "but I'm afraid I'll have to spend lunchtime grading my sophomore themes. I've fallen way behind recently—having trouble concentrating."

"Oh, I understand completely, George."

He turned to face her with an intense, compelling stare. George's recent drastic loss of weight had only improved his masculine good looks. Mary remembered the flash of his sculpted white chest and felt a sinuous clutch in her pelvic area.

"Besides," George said, "I promised Lauren I'd be faithful to her. If she sees me having lunch with a lovely female colleague . . . well, you know . . ."

Mary goggled at him. "That's an odd way of looking at it. I'm sure Lauren wouldn't mind at all. If I could cheer you up, she'd appreciate it."

George smiled. "It's kind of you to think of me, but really, I'm all right. I feel much better. I know I made a fool of myself yesterday, but now I think I've found a way to channel my mourning."

Mary, dubious, stared into George's calm green eyes and felt dazzled despite the dimness of the corridor.

"You see, last night, after I apologized for all my rottenness, and I really was rotten, Lauren forgave me. I felt a great weight lift from my heart."

"Oh, I'm so happy for you. That's wonderful. Don't be embarrassed. Everyone is rooting for you." She leaned closer and felt weaker.

George paid no attention. "I walked all the way home in the rain. I was soaked to the skin. I think I had a fever. When I reached my apartment, all the lights were burning and it was a loathsome mess, junk all over the floor. The garbage stank. When I opened up the broom closet to get some more food for my cats, Lauren was standing there in a cloud of white light. She talked to me for a long time very calmly, no recriminations. She wants to help me and now I know exactly what to do. She told me how to clean up my life. Specifically. In detail. She told me to pay more attention to my duties here at Muni."

Mary was too dumbfounded to do more than stare vacantly at George.

"I'm sure I can rely on you not to tell anyone. You're a discreet sort of person. I don't want to be a laughing-stock around here."

Mary nodded. George took a step away from her and hoisted his knapsack off his shoulder in a businesslike way. "And now, I'm afraid I must go to class and get on with my work."

"He's wandering around campus in an unstable mood," Quinton reported by telephone to the president's troubleshooter, Chuck Messerschmidt. "He told a colleague he had a heavenly vision of Lauren Goldberg telling him to do good works. God knows what he'll pull off next. Right now he's holed up in his office grading papers like a lunatic. I've tried to interview him, but I can't get hold of him except by phone. Says he's too busy to confer with me now. He's revamping all his syllabi and overhauling his book lists and rethinking his exams. Clearly he should be removed from classes and put on medical leave."

"That's not so easy to do," Messerschmidt replied in a rich, confident voice. "We're rather busy at the present time, so I can't review the legal aspects at length, but getting rid of a tenured professor is a very time-consuming procedure. I can send you some photocopied transcripts of previous cases, so you can see what I mean. Wearing funny clothes or making incoherent statements just ain't enough. He can do that till the cows come home. Has he threatened or tried to punch out any other faculty member? For the janitorial staff, drunk and disorderly is sufficient, but for the faculty we need violence."

"Look, he's deranged. He should be in an institution."

"You can't lock up someone because he's weird. This is America, Professor. For institutionalization you have to show he's going to harm himself or others. The police will tell you the same thing."

"That's ridiculous."

Messerschmidt's voice grew less emollient. "I don't make these procedures, as you know. Why don't you have a talk with Reilly and persuade him to take the semester off and seek treatment? He'll be paid, after all."

"It's very difficult to approach him. He thinks he's improving himself by these antics. He's polite. You'd swear he was sane. And no one here knows him that well, you know, in a personal way. Isn't there a university shrink he can speak to?"

"Budgetary constraints caused us to cut all psych services nine years ago."

3

The perk most prized by the English Chair wasn't his private secretary or reduced teaching schedule, but his spacious office with a double window and view of a special tree. This stunning pine tree was one of two beautiful sights on Muni campus (the other, a glimpse of office towers floating in the distance on certain days when the air was clear). In moments of urban stress the Chair liked to settle his gaze on the lush green boughs across the road and dream of his resignation and happy early retirement in East Hampton.

Tranquil days in his dream garden with the bees buzzing in the holly bush on the other side of the fence and a robin in the birdbath. No more conciliating angry professors. No more placating stingy administrators. No more contact with idiot students. No more Department of Buildings and Grounds.

Only a month ago the Department of Buildings and

Grounds had made a fatal error by widening the narrow road across from his window. No sooner was the traffic two-way than a reckless teenager went off the asphalt and crashed into the pine tree, wrecking his car, crippling himself, and leaving a sap-bleeding gash in the trunk.

On Thursday as the Chair sat at his desk, wondering how to attract a cheap visiting professor who was not an alcoholic or a Don Juan, two men came screeching up in a truck. They parked across from his window, slammed the doors, and emerged with a chain saw, a shovel, a broom, and several long dirty canvas straps with buckles on the ends. A huge black and tan Labrador-like dog jumped out of the back of the truck after them.

The Chair's powerful mind immediately foresaw the event. Shouting for Ramona, he ran out of his office and down the corridor, wheezing loudly as he went. He was fifty-four years old, and just now suffered cruelly from gout. He burst out the heavy glass door with a thump.

"What do you think you're doing?" he cried to the men, young but stumpy figures in baggy jeans. They gathered around him.

"Tree's got to come down," said the one he judged older because of his grizzled haircut, though he couldn't have been more than twenty-five.

"Who says?"

"Buildings and grounds."

"This is a fine old tree, older than the whole campus.

Nothing wrong with it except for a wound, which will heal up with proper attention by a tree surgeon."

"Sad thing," said the younger of the two thugs. He had a strangely literary appearance because he wore a dark dense D. H. Lawrence beard. "But it's not our responsibility. Boss says, cut it down."

"Ramona," the Chair bellowed. His secretary was hovering on the concrete doorstep of Temp 6, awaiting his commands. "Get buildings and grounds on the phone right away! Here—what are you doing?"

One of the men was climbing up on the roof of the cab, chain saw in hand. "Stop! Don't move till I talk to your superior."

D. H. Lawrence climbed down, put the chain saw on the ground and lit a cigarette. "We'll wait a coupla minutes," he said equably. He began patting his friendly dog. How was it *he* was allowed to keep an animal on campus? What was this, an institution of high learning, or some kind of shooting club? Even chairs of departments weren't allowed pets on campus.

When he saw Ramona beckoning from the window, the Chair hustled back inside and grabbed his phone. Bill Whitlock, the dark, good-looking head of buildings and grounds, had already irked the Chair when he gave a talk on landscaping the new library during the chancellor's last visit. It struck the Chair forcibly once again how easily tall good-looking men advanced in the world, while short round types like himself had to struggle, manipulate, and throw temper tantrums to get ahead.

"Who gave you permission to cut down that pine in front of my office?" he demanded.

"We cleared it with the president's office." Whitlock was forthright, unfazed. "It's a shame, I know—old tree—but it's a liability in case of a crash, a hazard in a narrow passage."

"Arrant nonsense! The tree's not a hazard, it's the drive that's too wide! Never mind. I'll talk to the president personally." The Chair slammed down the receiver. Narrow passage! Never mind. What did buildings and grounds count, after all? Who the hell was Bill Whitlock? In the greater academic world, he was no more than Lady Chatterley's lover.

The president's assistant, Chuck Messerschmidt, by now an old acquaintance, answered the Chair's query in a more soothing, sympathetic voice, but the message was just as disagreeable.

"I understand your concern. But you know we have to avoid the appearance of negligence. We consulted the university lawyers, big liability experts."

"If the driver stays on the road, there's no chance of a collision."

"It's a tough call. I know you want to make your feelings known. Just between the two of us, the president is gung ho on negligence. Do you want me to put you through to him? He's in a really testy mood today. You should have heard him chewing out Crostini a while ago." Messerschmidt made a cracking noise in his throat, signifying summary court martial and execution.

The Chair thought for a second. His appeal on the budget cuts lay on the president's desk at this moment. "No thanks."

Drat! The Chair hung up the receiver, rose to his feet, and threw open the window. He called, "Go ahead! Chop away! Do your worst!" Then he sat down at his desk to watch. Though he'd given up the habit twelve years ago, he strongly craved a Marlboro.

Standing casually on the roof of the cab, Lawrence pulled the cord to start his chain saw. In a few minutes he cut off five of the smaller branches, neatly managing to knock the limbs directly into the open bed of the truck below. Then he passed his saw down to Grizzle, who stood in the truck sawing limbs into manageable size. The Chair noted the easy cooperation between the two men, who didn't stop for conferences or prolonged bickering, but arranged matters quickly with a few words. "Over here?" "Too close."

Grizzle passed the chain saw back up to Lawrence, who climbed monkeylike into the higher branches. The Chair sat up, horrified at the nonchalant way Lawrence moved around in the tree, a foot in one crotch, another a foot or so higher, perilous perch for starting a chain saw.

The Chair had heard that these machines were dangerous and must be handled with care to prevent horrible mutilations. He felt a moment of panic and opened the window again. "Hey," he shouted. "It's not going to crash on our building here, is it?"

Lawrence grinned. "Hope not."

Even without its lower branches, the pine remained magnificent, limbs bristling with glossy green needles. Lawrence tied the canvas belt around the upper limbs, then slowly sawed each one off, while Grizzle held the belt from the ground. Reaching forward, taking fearful chances, shifting his weight and bending far beyond his precarious platform, Lawrence removed one, two, three, four limbs within a lithe acrobat's reach. The Chair felt uneasy as each weight toppled down. Surely you were supposed to hold a chain saw close to your body.

Occasionally a car drove past, and the two men stopped work to let it inch by. When all possible limbs had been stripped away and cut into logs, Lawrence climbed way, way up. He wrapped the canvas belt around the topmost trunk with a certain degree of caution. Peering closely, he made two neat cuts on the righthand side. Grizzle held fast to the end of the strap on the ground, muttering, "Slow, man, slow. Watch it, watch it."

Lawrence made one more neat cut, and, with spellbinding precision, the branch-heavy top crashed right smack into the back of the truck.

The Chair felt like calling "Bravo!" but he was afraid to say a word. Now the tree was a wreck—a hulk without meaning or charm. Standing on the roof of the cab, Lawrence made three more cuts and the midsection crashed, too. Grizzle grabbed the saw, started it up again and, leaning the trunk over a log, swiftly sawed it into chunks. Lawrence, back down on the ground, tossed the logs into the truck. His short graceful figure seemed to be dancing around out there.

Now for the stump, taller than Lawrence himself. He worked diligently for a while with his three-cut routine. Over it went. While Grizzle sawed, Lawrence shoveled earth away from the stub, which now protruded a few inches above the ground. Then he shot the nose of the saw into the stub, reducing it to a powerful spray of sawdust.

His prized tree was gone, a truckful of splinters and sticks, yet the Chair was surprised to find himself exhilarated. He felt like leaping up and shouting. "Man against nature," he mused to himself, liking the sound.

The groundsmen were scurrying around in a wide circle, one picking up scraps of cone, the other furiously sweeping sawdust and bark chips. Overcome by impulse, the Chair opened his window and cried at the top of his voice, "Man against nature!"

The two men tipped their caps.

With pine needles and dirt neatly shoveled over the

site, there was no sign that a tree had ever stood across the road. Looking less baggy and stumpy, the workers dumped their tools in the back of the truck. The dog, barking loudly, leaped into the cab with them, and they drove off with a screech. Less than an hour had passed.

On his desk the Chair had a great pile of teaching contracts for next fall to sign, but he didn't take up his pen. He sat and stared out the window with longings he couldn't quite pin down.

P & B member Dickie Walter entered the ESF elevator in a flutter of impatience and jabbed the up button several times. He was dying to get upstairs to Daphne with his wonderful news. Only this morning he'd received a letter from Harvard summer school, asking him to teach nineteenth-century fiction. A Harvard graduate of the fifties, he'd been waiting his whole life long for a summons from his alma mater. As the elevator doors slowly inched open at the third floor, Dickie felt like pushing them apart with his bare hands and bursting through.

Daphne wasn't in her office. How irritating. He moved up the corridor to knock on Maurice el-Okdah's door. Murray, a fellow Harvard graduate, was out as well. Dickie scuttled around the corner and tried Lucille. No response—a conspiracy of silence.

As he passed the men's room, Steve Somebody, a lecturer, emerged, a sort of dim shabby individual, but an ear nonetheless. "Halloo, Steve!" Dickie said, and the young man shambled to a stop. "I've just heard this morning I'm to teach nineteenth-century fiction at Harvard summer school!"

"That's awfully good news—you must be delighted," Steve Somebody said with a shy smile.

Dickie felt very pleased with himself. "I am, and I'm already planning my syllabus. The only question is—are they ready for *Daniel Deronda*, even at Harvard summer school? Dickens, Thackeray, Trollope, shall I add Gissing? Can I beef up my usual reading list for those high-powered surroundings?"

"It's only summer school," Steve replied. "I doubt they're that exalted. It's not nearly as selective as the regular session."

"Hmf," Dickie snorted, not bothering to end the conversation but charging off in the opposite direction.

By the time of the meeting of the P & B Committee that afternoon, Dickie had almost forgotten this unpleasant encounter. A chorus of congratulations wiped the memory away. "Their nineteenth-century man has nephritis," he reported happily to everyone he met. "They thought immediately of me. Of course it will mean lots of extra work and Cambridge *is* dreadfully hot in summer, but you know I'm devoted to the place."

Indeed, Dickie still carried a genuine fifties Harvard book bag from the Coop, a sturdy, ugly blackish-green sack with an olive webbed strap. In absolute mint condition. He'd bought a lifetime supply.

The Personnel and Budget Committee didn't meet very often, considering the momentous questions of hiring and firing disposed of during its sessions. The setting was squalid, a windowless committee room in the basement of the library, stuffy and choked with ancient dust. The committee had abandoned the little seminar room in Temp 6 because the walls were too thin. Daphne, on her way to the ladies', found Allen Swain stooping at the water fountain to hear every detail of their secret deliberations.

Today was a crucial meeting, for the department, despite crying wolf many times earlier, really did have big budget woes. The Chair was the last to arrive, red-faced and huffing a little from the steep library stairs, carrying his Ralph Lauren blazer foulard lining outward in a little packet to preserve it from the dust.

"My apologies. Today of all days, a conflict with the provost's reception. I must leave at 4:10 sharp," he began with a weary smile. "I've been reviewing staff sheets and been on the line with the vice-chancellor's office all afternoon without a moment's respite."

"Lucille won't be here today," Daphne interrupted. "She has the Task Force on Remediation." This semester Lucille was pinch-hitting for P & B member Harve Proctor, who was on Fulbright in Sydney, Australia.

"Oh, good," the Chair responded absentmindedly. He cleared his throat, trying to find appropriate words.

"Disquieting news. My massive efforts to retain our present funding have been unavailing. Since the administration won't release sufficient funds to enable us to cover our present staffing needs, we must trim our sheets to the wind." His hearers understood what he meant—we're too weak to threaten them. "Now our number cruncher, Daphne, will give us a budget overview."

Daphne didn't fool around. She turned once in her oak swivel chair to look each member in the eye, creating a little shiver in all. "The news is catastrophic. All the nonessential cuts were made in the seventies. Now it's cuts to the bone.

"Without offering tenure to a single candidate, we'll still have a shortfall. Our first step is to cut all our yearly and part-time people. Send them a letter this week so the administration knows we mean business. Fire now, hire back in the fall, if any funds come through. My guess is that they *will* come through. Historically the city always manages to find some money."

"We should make the letter a little optimistic about the future," Quinton put in, "or they'll take other jobs."

"I doubt it. They've been through budget crises before. They'll collect unemployment over the summer and wait till September. The alternative is too gruesome."

"What about staffing our freshman classes?"

"Increasing class size by eight should take care of the shortfall," Daphne said crisply. "As you know, our serious difficulty comes with full-time professorships. At the moment, Lauren's line is our only resource and we've several prospects up for tenure. My own inclination is just to transfer the line to Brian McGlinchee without wasting valuable time. His scholarship is excellent, and it would be a great pity to let him go after all he's done for the department. He's been very helpful, very enthusiastic, I must say. Staying late, coming in early. Doing good work, Brian."

Muffled comments of "good fellow," "let's give it to him" were going around the table when Quinton broke in again. "If Lauren's line isn't filled by someone in her field, who'll cover modern poetry? Brian is a Renaissance man."

A pause while this sound idea sank in.

"Any other possible lines available?" Quinton asked.

"Lou Fishman is making retirement noises. Can we shove him a little?"

"How?"

"Give him a freshman class, late afternoon and evening schedule."

"What a stink he'll make."

"So!"

"Better speak to Brian about scheduling it, but Lou is a pretty stubborn coot. It's a long shot."

"If Murray moves up to the graduate center, that will free up his line. He applied for a distinguished professorship, but I doubt he'll be approved."

"How's Murray's book?"

"Long."

"But otherwise?"

"Otherwise a rehash of his first groundbreaking study. But do we really want to lose Murray? Can we get by without him? We need somebody for African-American, or the students will riot. You know black professors are scarcer than hen's teeth."

"Still, we'll have a couple of terms to search for a replacement, and the money will be flowing again by then."

"What about Cherry Binder?" Quinton spoke in his most booming voice. "I'm surprised you've omitted mention of Cherry. I've always assumed her promotion and tenure were automatic. Her work is distinguished without question. Brian is a nonentity beside her."

Quinton flipped open the pale pink folder before him and shuffled through the thick sheaf of papers. Everyone else dutifully pulled folders on Cherry in a great shower of motes. The room was hot and stuffy, filled with sighs.

"I'm sure you've all read *Cries from the Green Country: Wives Who Write*, which Josephine Partridge in *The New York Times Book Review*, page 4, called 'seminal.' John Drone gave her a rave in *The Atlantic*." Quinton waved the photocopied pages, which gave a good satisfying rattle. "She was nominated for an Evergreen Award for women scholars under forty. This line by rights belongs to Cherry. Just look at this list of top-tier publications. She's indefatigable. All we must do is ask her to teach one course in modern poetry in addition to women's studies. It fits in with our budgetary constraints, and I can't see any bar to it. I'm sure you agree." He settled back in his chair with a heavy, satisfied grunt.

Daphne pushed the folder away with a sour smile. "Let me enlighten you about Cherry's plans, Quinton. You know her husband received tenure at SMU last year? Well, she's just waiting for her tenure here to transfer to a professorship with tenure *there*."

"Who told you that? You must be joking!" Quinton jerked his head up, irked. He'd been acting as Cherry's mentor for years, and she'd never mentioned such a move.

"I'm not. I had it from a reliable member of the department. Cherry is just using the department. As soon as she gets that tenure, mark my words, she'll be off like a shot to SMU."

"It's not unheard of," Quinton said judiciously, determined to back Cherry. "I did the same thing at LSU. She's taught here for six years successfully; we owe her something. How do you know about Southern Methodist, anyway? It's probably idle gossip."

"Mary Burnson told me. Word of honor. Strictest

confidence. Her correspondence was mixed, that is, Cherry's letter fell into her pigeonhole by mistake and was accidentally opened."

"Quinton, there's something you're probably not aware of," Dickie added. "Cherry's been bringing her baby to school. I've heard loud gurgling coming from her office. She's nursing the child in there, Murry says."

"Resourceful, very resourceful," Quinton said, but in a less confident tone. "She doesn't take the baby to class, does she? Has anyone complained?"

"Gets a student to sit for her. Still, there's got to be a racket. Babies cry. Matter of time. She's coming to school with diapers in her briefcase, she's not using her office for conferences anymore, but for . . . breast-feeding!"

Quinton shook his massive head sadly. "I'm surprised to hear it. That does indeed change my view. If she's breast-feeding on our premises instead of attending to her professional duties, we don't owe her anything."

"Okay, we'll drop her," the Chair said in evident relief, glad the discussion was moving along briskly. It was five minutes to four. "But she's a strong candidate and I know she'll appeal our decision. How can we be sure she won't win? The administration doesn't want any long drawn-out appeals. A successful appeal merits back pay, you know. We'll look like flats if that happens."

"Is there anything negative in her file?"

"Not a thing. There's nothing in the bylaws about breast-feeding," Daphne said primly.

They all sat brainstorming for half a minute, till Dickie brightened. "I know! Get Lucille to check on her evening class," he suggested. "Most of those night people are dismissing class way early. They don't have the stamina to go the full two and a half hours. Get Lucille to go in at 10:15 and see if Cherry is still in her classroom."

"Great idea! If we're going to vote officially tomorrow, it should be done tonight, so Lucille had better get on the stick. Oh—make sure she checks on everybody, gets lots of names, otherwise it'll look as if we're out specifically to get Cherry." The Chair stood up, unwrapped his packet, and began struggling into his blazer. He looked a little more cheerful. "I must dash, so we'd better close for the moment. Tomorrow, same time, and let's pencil in another meeting for the twenty-fifth."

They all breathed sighs of relief and began moving away from the conference table.

"I'm bushed."

"This work takes its toll. So many important decisions."

When Quinton flung open the door, the flickering fluorescent light in the passage cast an ugly light on the committee. "You know," he said, "I was just thinking. If Lauren hadn't died, we'd be in big trouble."

That evening Steve craved wheels. He stopped by ESF 101 a few minutes before eight to ask for a lift, but Cherry had already begun her lecture. He peeped through the window at her stout figure stomping back and forth in front of the class; she'd gained about forty pounds with Morley and hadn't dropped them yet.

Wearing her maternity clothes and high-heeled cowboy boots, gesticulating and shaking her great mane of dark hair, she was obviously in high gear; she must be planning to dismiss early tonight. Was she going to take the usual ten-minute break, or would she skip it and leave even earlier?

The classroom was packed. Some of her students were staring at her transfixed, while others had their hands full transcribing her rapid-fire disclosures about Rebecca Harding Davis's *Life in the Iron Mills*. On the side blackboard was a bold orange scrawl: IRON MILLS—LIFE!

Steve stood outside the door for a while, wondering what to do. Perhaps Cherry would glance his way and see him through the window. At that moment she wheeled and pointed her finger menacingly at the class. Steve watched her with fascination, wishing he felt confident enough to cavort like this in the classroom. He usually sat tightly clenched behind his teacher's desk, hoping to avoid disaster.

Steve decided to go to Cherry's office and leave a message with the baby-sitter. No matter what time Cherry left Muni campus, Steve wanted to be with her. He'd had a nagging headache since before his conference hour, and planned to have his freshman class write impromptu essays to spare him a tiring classroom discussion. But how could he assign a writing topic if he didn't know how long the class would last? It wouldn't be fair to the slow starters if he snatched their papers away at an instant's notice, and he knew from experience that Cherry wouldn't wait for him.

He ran upstairs to the third floor and knocked on Cherry's office door. Nobody answered. Maybe Morley hadn't come to school tonight. He tried the door handle. It opened easily. The baby-sitter must be in the ladies' because Morley was asleep in the filing cabinet drawer. Steve watched from the threshold for a moment with a smile on his face, then gently closed the door; his class was waiting for him.

Once they had begun writing about "Paul's Case" (not without many protests), he dashed back up to Cherry's office to find Morley still asleep and still no baby-sitter. Had Cherry really left her child alone? Had the sitter absconded? He thought for a minute, trying to decide what to do.

That's why when Lucille Streng came to check on the faculty around 10:15, she found Steve Speck sitting in his classroom watching three late-writing stragglers with a baby on his chest. She was so dumbfounded that she barged right in and berated him instead of simply recording his bizarre behavior in her notes. As for Cherry Binder, she was nowhere to be found.

•

How glad Cherry was that the elevator in ESF was slow. Locked in passionate embrace with Sally Gonzalez of the French department, feeling Sally's soft fingers slipping under her bra and cupping her milk-swollen breasts, Cherry was trembling in ecstasy and also in anxiety and fear.

What if the doors suddenly opened and she was caught by some stuffy colleague with her active ardent tongue in Sally's mouth? Despite this unsettling image, she couldn't bring herself to step away from Sally, bonded to her in one corner of the elevator as if by Krazy Glue.

"Let's go to my office," Sally mumbled into her cheek. "Just across the quad."

"What about Morley?"

"Yolanda will watch him."

"No, she can't. She has another job after this. I can't do it. I need her all semester." Cherry closed her eyes and dug her hands under the elastic of Sally's panty hose, caressing her firm flat belly. She imagined licking her smooth olive skin. "Let's get Morley and go to my house. We can wait an hour."

"Can we?"

When the door opened at the third floor, the dim corridor was empty. Cherry peered out, still holding fast to Sally, who was just her height, solid, round, warm, authentic. Dragging Sally back towards the elevator panel, she pushed the down button and again fell into ecstasy.

One more slow dangerous trip down. Cherry felt slightly crazy. Who could ever explain the strength of this attraction, the pull like a tropism to Sally's luscious firm-fleshed body? "Let's get Morley and get out of here."

When they reached Cherry's office, the little cell was empty. On top of the diaper bag was a note scribbled on a mimeographed notice. "Cherry: no baby-sitter! Have Morley in 203—Steve."

"Oh, hell. What happened to Yolanda?"

"It's early yet. Class won't be over for ages. Please, let's go to my office. That's Steve Speck, the lecturer, isn't it? The baby is safe with him. He's harmless, lover."

"Mmm."

"He won't mind waiting. Please. Oh, please, Cherry, please, please."

Steve was sunk in gloom, stung by Lucille's angry words. How had he managed to stumble so badly when he was trying so hard to be good? Now he was in trouble—not charged with going AWOL from the classroom like his unlucky colleagues, but caught holding the baby. Would he lose his job over this? Someone who enjoyed reading and writing and working in the library stacks—why couldn't they leave him alone? Why couldn't he live freely—like his hero, Henry Martin? The austere poet held no ties to wife, children, or even to his country, going his own way . . . to the point of disappearing!

Steve gave a sudden snort. Angry as he was with Lucille, he was also furious with Cherry and with her son, this little breathing lump on his shoulder, the cause of his humiliation. Morley was starting to smell bad.

To be scolded in front of his students, sitting down in front of that ranting harpy, caught like some kindergartner wetting his pants! Morley, to his credit, slept peacefully on, but what would Steve do when he woke hungry for his mother's milk? Steve stood up gingerly and paced to the blackboard and back. Class had been over for twenty minutes.

Captain Jack, the elderly security guard in shiny blue uniform, poked his head in the door. "Still here?"

"God Almighty! Do you think I'm taking this baby home with me? Am I going to adopt him?" What would Aimee say if he brought home an infant? She was living with him full-time now, her parents approving enough to help with the rent. He doubted she was ready for child care.

"My wife forgot two of my kids," offered Captain Jack, "two separate times. Left one behind at the supermarket, 'nother one sleeping in her stroller in a friend's yard. Happens all the time, forgetting a kid. Ladies got a lot on their minds, especially that one."

"God Almighty," Steve muttered.

"Just sit here peaceful. I got to lock the building

soon. Then you come sit in the security office. Have some coffee. I've got some smokes." He winked.

At that moment Cherry rushed in, larger than life, her face rosy with anxiety.

"Oh, Steve, I'm so sorry. What a stupid thing to happen!"

Steve always hated conflict with other people. What did it accomplish, after all? If he told Cherry what he thought of her harebrained actions, how would it help? He'd lose his only campus friend, that's all.

"Did you see Lucille?"

"Did I! Oh, my God! I met her in the vestibule. She looked like the avenging angel. I told her my class had enjoyed two satisfying hours of tip-top education, but she just sputtered in my face. What the hell! Who cares about that battle-ax? How's my sweet baby? Give him to me."

She lifted Morley into her sheltering arms. He woke up, fussed, and began whimpering.

"Oh, are you wet! Couldn't you change him, Steve?"

Cherry sat down in the teacher's chair, lifted her smock, and with a beatific expression began nursing.

Alert observers from the English department were surprised to see Cherry Binder and Allen Swain lunching at a table for two in a semisecluded corner of the faculty lunchroom, their gazes locked. With the table hiding Allen's elfin figure and Cherry's powerful bulk, their two handsome faces staring magnetically at each other across the Formica suggested a meeting of lovers rather than a cabal.

"Five of us have disciplinary notes in our files, but I'm the one they were out to get," Cherry told Allen.

"Outrageous! I never heard of such gross manipulation. For a long time I've felt the present regime was out of bounds, but this—" Allen waved his fork in the air, then stabbed the tough crust of his chicken pie. "Beyond belief!"

"I'm going to reveal everything at the next department meeting," Cherry said. "Let *everyone* know what happened to me. I'm not going to be stabbed in the back without an outcry."

"You'll never get on the agenda," Allen murmured, glancing suspiciously around at the neighboring tables filled, fortunately, with science faculty. "Naive to think so. The most you can hope to accomplish on your own is a grievance with the union."

Cherry shook her thick dark hair impatiently. "I've already telephoned the local chairman. He's the former bio chair, so it's hard to see him as a defender of faculty rejects. He's going to look at my file. He sounded noncommittal."

Allen leaned forward. "Another way to proceed is just to throw the rascals out," he said quietly.

"Throw the rascals out?"

"A challenge at the departmental election."

"But it's not time for a change yet. The incumbent chair always serves a second term."

"Who says?" Allen cocked his head and affected a leer. In his heart he thought of Humphrey Bogart as Duke Mantee. "It will be a fight, but in the spirit of revolt I'm ready to offer myself as a candidate."

Cherry laughed. "You don't have a chance!"

"Perhaps not. Perhaps yes. I have a number of friends among the junior faculty—people whom I've helped and advised over the past few years. I've gone out of my way to nurture them. Folks without tenure prefer a new regime."

"The junior people can't afford to risk their jobs."

"I have the numbers." Allen reached inside his vest and took out a little yellow Post-it dense with names. "These are my sure supporters. I've counseled all these assistant professors, found them better committee assignments, that sort of thing. I've even revised grant applications." He handed it to Cherry, who looked impressed.

She studied it carefully and looked up with a glint in her eyes. "I'll join you, of course. I'm already axed, and have nothing to lose."

"I welcome your support." Allen nodded. "Formidable support. An excellent associate chair you'd make. But we must act intelligently. We have one chance only. If we lose this spring, most of our supporters will be gone by the next election."

"What do I do?"

"First, spread the word about the Wednesday Night Massacre. Spare no details. How you were out buying baby formula."

"I'd rather not bring Morley into this."

"Well, focus on Lucille's stalking you the very night before your tenure decision. The first time anyone ever checked up in this way."

"People teaching day classes won't be that sympathetic. They can't leave early. Too conspicuous. Besides, no one with tenure will dare take a chance on you."

"Don't be too sure. There are plenty of disgruntled senior people: the insulted, the passed over, the malicious. And it's not simply a matter of leaves and promotions and good schedules and bad schedules. You can see the department is turning into Big Brother. No one is safe. They'll be checking to see if Allen Swain is keeping his office hours, and if Cherry Binder assigned all her papers."

Cherry smiled. "It sounds wonderful—faculty freedom. But, I repeat, no one with tenure will take a chance on you."

"Don't be too sure." Allen leaned forward and regarded her with his alert gaze. "Change is often very seductive."

"No, it's not. Everything boils down to leaves and promotions, and nobody wants to risk the future. If the P & B hadn't attacked me, I wouldn't be here with you now. I'd be trying to get on the P & B. You know that, Allen." She gave him a tender look.

Allen returned the compliment. "We understand each other, at least. It's a rare thing. Also, Cherry, are you aware that Quinton is considering an offer to head the graduate program at NYU? He may be leaving soon."

"Who told you that? Is that true?"

"A little bird told me. But don't spread that one around, please. It may give ideas to other candidates."

"Okay. Let's start the campaign right away. I'll foment as best I can. I'll start circulating in the faculty lounge this afternoon. Shall I also try the graduate assistants' room?"

"Don't bother. They have no vote."

4

A cold night in December. The ground in the quad was hard frozen. The four trees on campus were bare. Steam pounded the faulty radiators. In the scuffed corridor of the humanities building, near the bulletin board awash with jumbled notices, a knot of English teachers huddled together while their students evaluated them. In the harsh fluorescent light the refugees seemed pale and drawn.

"Thrown out of your own classroom! What lunacy! These student questionnaires are ridiculous. Wastes our time. Nobody ever looks at them," Harry Rhett declared with an aristocratic toss of his head.

"Not quite." Mary Burnson, doyenne of the group, was eager to set him straight. "Daphne told me that if two candidates are in a dead heat for one job the P & B will definitely consider how their students rate them."

"These questionnaires, is it permissible to see

them?" Igor Blavatsky asked, nervously tugging at his suit sleeve. "Is self-improving possible?"

"Of course. You request to have the comments typed. You get them back about a year later when you can't even remember the class, let alone recognize the handwriting."

"In the first class I taught, only two people bothered to comment," Harry complained, "and the kind person was illiterate."

"No one takes them seriously. Everyone gets pounded," Heidi Weismuller said.

"They really give it to you," Betsy Fuller put in.

"Not completely true. I understand that Lauren Goldberg always got rave reviews."

Silence. As if by unspoken agreement the group drifted away from each other in twos and threes.

Later in ESF 101, Brian McGlinchee looked at the manila envelopes of evaluation forms on his desk and felt a stab of panic. He'd forgotten all about this whimsical ritual.

His students had every right to complain about him. English 29 had been slipping away from him ever since he'd begun sleeping with Cynthia. Everything had been slipping away.

You couldn't take the teenage girls that seriously, no matter how they twitched their asses. But Cynthia Lovitt was a grown-up woman, maybe older than he was. No desirable woman had ever pursued him before. Why did she want him?

In the first weeks of the term Cynthia affected to be confused about Middle English and Chaucer, but her essays were excellent, shrewd and polished. Daytimes Cynthia worked for a magazine as a researcher. Digging up the dirt, she called it. For some unexplained reason, she'd never gotten her BA. Some mystery in her past.

He'd first noticed her sitting alone at the back of the room during break. He'd been mesmerized by her supper—a paper carton of six large shrimp on a bed of noodles which she dipped delicately with chopsticks in a little container of soy sauce and munched without spilling a drop. Most students ate taco chips, at best a greasy hamburger from the student cafeteria. He decided to ignore the shrimps, their effect on him. At this point in his career it was madness to get involved with a student.

Brian picked up the evaluations and weighed their heft. He felt headachy. Both the twins had had earaches and high fever all night long, and the pediatrician hadn't called back till after breakfast. Tiffany kept waking him up with her hand-wringing and moaning. She dragged back and forth ceaselessly across the bedroom in her shapeless blood-red bathrobe.

Cynthia was so tiny and shapely. Her hair was puffed high in ringlets, her head bigger than her chest, which for a small girl was considerable.

She wore long skirts which made her look tinier and military-looking silk shirts in luscious citrus colors with gleaming buttons tucked into her minuscule waist. Expensive high-heeled boots. A chic commanding officer.

She was divorced from Lovitt, a shady Australian. Upwardly mobile. Her maiden name D'Angelo. A ten-year-old son who was away at Cathedral School on full scholarship. Wonderful soprano voice he had, at least for the time being.

Lovely Cynthia gave him stock market tips direct from her boss, not that Brian could afford to invest. Her apartment in Windemere Gardens was sparsely furnished, but all very expensive stuff. Not like Tiffany's Sears Roe-buck taste. A polished sleigh bed, that got him. Why did she want him?

Now students were drifting singly into class. They weren't social, part of a herd, like day students. Tired out, straight from work, frowns of concentration rather than spaced-out blanks. In trotted Cynthia. He nodded from his desk. They always greeted each other, hypocritical to ignore. Her hips swayed confidently. The other women were brutish in comparison; she knew it, too. Her heels clicked in superiority.

A pity this semester was going badly. Attendance slipping, little class response. If it hadn't been for Cynthia, his classroom observation by the P & B would have been dismal. She'd bailed him out with a few well-chosen remarks and questions, so it seemed a lively class. Dickie

Walter had been utterly fooled. No one in this survey course was ever willing to talk; even Cynthia hung back, except on the night he was observed. She didn't want to seem overeager?

His headache was worsening. These goddamn evaluations were supposed to take twenty minutes. Good. His lecture notes were skimpy tonight. Jacobean World Picture, not his favorite topic. If he got his tenure, he might never have to teach survey again. Ten people in their seats. A quorum. The hard-core tough nuts were all here. Harley Feldschuh, the motorcycle brute. Luis Pisarro, the Marxist critic. Ahmed Akbar, the sleeper. Four indistinguishable white girls, two black.

Jovial smile. "Student evaluations tonight. I know you've been waiting for the chance to grade me." Smile, smiles from all but Pisarro. "Please use number two pencils for the short answers and write legibly on the written comments. For the next twenty minutes I'll be upstairs in my office."

He had a tiny moment of doubt before he said, "Ms. Lovitt, will you take charge, please? Distribute the forms, deliver them to the English office after class."

She gave him a little complicitous smile as he made for the door. He could ask her to show them to him when they met at her car. Why not? It wouldn't take a minute, and he was curious.

It was hard to find a parking place on Muni campus, but Cynthia usually managed to ferret one out. After class Brian spotted her in the very darkest back lot by the silhouette of her 1979 Saab, which stood out from the Fords and Toyotas. Because his own car was being repaired, Cynthia had offered to drive him home.

They embraced on the dark front seat. Brian felt thwarted by the thick fabric of Cynthia's jacket. He fumbled the buttons open only to be confronted by another set of smaller buttons and then another silky layer. He caressed Cynthia's thin vulnerable shoulders and heavy, big-nippled breasts. "Let's stop at your place," he said in a monotone, fingering the nipples. There was no way, even in the comfortable Saab seats, to join their lower bodies.

"Won't that make you late?"

"No."

"I'm supposed to drop those papers off at the English office."

"It's late. You can do it tomorrow."

At Cynthia's they tumbled about in her Empire sleigh bed for a long time. Brian had remarkable staying power, and Cynthia enjoyed it, calling out in a demanding voice at each exertion. "For an English teacher, you are one great lover," she told him when they'd sunk down together on the king-size pillow.

"Thanks," Brian mumbled into Cynthia's breast while still half conscious. She brushed at his face, then turned and drew the down comforter around her. Silence for a little while. Soon Brian dragged himself up from darkness and dreams of giant baby contorted faces, green vomit on a cotton diaper.

The yellow numerals of the bedside clock said 11:15. Brian turned on the light and put on his glasses. On the bedside table lay the manila envelope. He couldn't resist shuffling through. Clever Cynthia hadn't sealed the envelope.

Each evaluation form had two parts, a short-answer section of six questions and a brief space for handwritten remarks. Of the ten students present, only three had bothered to comment. The first was bland.

Most students taking this course, I believe have practically no knowledge of literature. Therefore the literature that is introduced to them should not be at a very deep level. If the students feels he or she is interested enough more advanced courses could be taken in which the depth of poetry could be pursued. The instructor was prefessional but cold.

Brian shook his head. Propping himself higher on the pillow he moved on to the second comment.

I feel Prof. McGlinchee teached the course extremely badly. He possess a poor quality teaching technique that don't encourage students to excel. Mainly he's boreing, a real ternoff.

Brian clenched his teeth in annoyance. After ten years of graduate study, he was still teaching illiterates. Was that sparkling prose style the work of Harley Feldschuh, who had the engine block number of his motorcycle tattooed on his forearm? Brian popped out of bed and walked naked to his briefcase, which was in the corner by the door. He brought it back to bed and began burrowing through an enormous sheaf of papers.

His rattling woke Cynthia, who poked her upper body from the covers. "What are you doing, darling? Grading papers in bed? Have we come to that?"

Brian absentmindedly patted her shoulder. "Just checking something," he said. He was searching for the midterms he'd been carrying around for weeks. He seized on a crushed blue book and began perusing it. Yes, yes— Harley Feldschuh. Those bubbling blots! The swollen letters! He wrote with a sticky hairy ballpoint—the sticky hairy brute. "F" was much too kind a fate.

He turned to the last evaluation. This one really hurt.

Instructor conveyed a lot of "knowledge" of interpreting literature and poetry, but method of interaction with students made class unpleasant. Instructor seemed to lack an ounce of enthusiasm or interest in students' development or grasp of material or interest, seemed burned out and contemptuous of students. Perhaps a respite from undergraduates, or some revelatory interactions with students would redeem some caring for us novices.

"Let me see now, let me see . . . ," Brian muttered.

"Just what are you doing, Brian?"

But Brian was too busy matching up the whorls and

loops of these thin slanting letters with the words in a blue book belonging to one Iris Blatt. He shook his head without answering. Who the hell was Iris Blatt?

"What's going on? Marking in your sleep? Are you alive?"

"I'm just taking a peek at these evaluations," Brian replied, wholly absorbed in his search, groping in his briefcase for his gradebook. Whining Iris Blatt had earned the grade of B+ with a little red asterisk that meant "promising," though he couldn't remember the title of her essay, or its subject.

Cynthia mischievously reached for Brian's penis. "If you *are* alive, perhaps we can rouse little Scotty to action?"

Turning slightly to protect himself from her prying hands, Brian ran his eyes down the short-answer results: *What is your overall evaluation of the instructor as distinct from the course?* Excellent—1, Very Good—0, Good—1, Fair—2, Poor—6.

"No, this is god-awful! I can't believe this," Brian cried, sitting bolt upright. "Did you take a look at these? Six students thought I was *poor*."

"They *are* pretty stupid," Cynthia said with a smile. "C'mon, let's do it again. Give little Scotty a chance."

Brian glanced at another question, his ruddy cheeks flushing even redder. *Would you advise another student to take this course with this instructor?* Definitely—1, Probably—0, Maybe—1, I doubt it—3, Definitely not—5.

"I appear completely incompetent. What if the P & B looks at this? The course isn't going *that* badly, is it?" Without waiting for a reply, Brian seized a number two pencil from the pocket of his briefcase and furiously erased black marks from little blue circles.

"Don't, darling." Giving up on verbal appeal, Cynthia began caressing his naked well-upholstered back and licking his thick powerful neck. Usually one lick was enough.

"Look, Cynthia," he said, defensively wiggling his back. "In a class this size every negative rating is a disaster."

"It's not that important, lover. Don't get so upset."

But Brian kept on erasing.

And what about George? He was standing near the front door of his apartment muttering to himself. For weeks now he'd been looking for his winter coat. Repeated hunts through his closets failed to unearth it. He couldn't remember taking it to the cleaners last spring. In fact, last spring seemed distant as his boyhood.

"Where? Where? Where did I put it?" He recalled wearing the coat, a handsome loden green duffle with a leather collar, on a clandestine trip to Montauk with Lauren during spring vacation. The coat always made him feel self-assured and prosperous. "Aren't we the landed gentry?" Lauren had said with her wonderful smile, but after that, who could remember? Perhaps he'd left the coat in a restaurant or at the tennis club. Now he was wearing an Irish fisherman's sweater topped with a red nylon windbreaker. Perhaps that's why he'd stopped going out unless absolutely necessary.

A peep through his front window at Hampton Place showed cracking wind, dim clouded light, passersby swaddled in scarves and parkas. Groping at the back of the hall closet, George pulled out his old orange-and-black Princeton scarf. He wound it twice about his head and shoulders, then stepped cautiously out into the December blast.

Farm Fresh was almost empty, the deli section drafty and deserted. The slender dark man behind the counter, who was smoking a cigarette and reading the sports section on the cutting block, used to be a garrulous acquaintance. Now, after not seeing George for a while, he greeted him with a cool nod.

George felt wounded and shifted uneasily from foot to foot. The trouble was he wasn't hungry. He'd only ventured out because he couldn't stand the rotting food in the refrigerator. He stared without appetite at the bloody meats and technicolor salads in the display case. Curried chicken salad, $4.50 1/4 lb., a bilious yellow mess. Daily special, tender stuffed vine leaves, squalid little green turds.

"Next!" the counterman said impatiently.

"Roast beef on rye with lettuce and tomato."

The cutter gleamed, the shining knife flicked once, then twice.

"Mustard?"

"No, thanks." George paused. "What's the matter, Ottilio, you don't recognize me?"

"Sure. What's new. You ain't been in for long time."

"Not much. Busy, very busy."

In a minute George was on the street again with a little brown paper bag. "Dirty, dismal place. Ugly, diseased."

Muttering to himself, George left the bustle of Main Street to turn into the backwater of Hampton Place, walking toward the squat two-family house where he rented the ground floor. Suddenly George saw a huge dog moving ahead of him on the sidewalk at a good clip, a handsome creature with abundant black fur standing in a ruff, a sled dog. For a large animal he had an odd rickety gait, his hind legs moving in stiff rotation as if they were hurting.

When the dog stopped to sniff a garbage can at the curb, George understood that the creature was lost and hungry. As it wandered on, George followed.

When the animal paused to sniff another garbage can, George suddenly ripped open the paper bag he was carrying and pulled the hunk of red beef from the bread. "Here's food," he called, but the dog only glanced at him sideways and trotted onward, his hind quarters racketing back and forth in that disturbing way.

George bypassed his own house, trailing just a few yards behind the dog, letting out frosty breath and still waving the roast beef. After half a block, the animal moved into an alleyway and lay down. George hesitated at the mouth of the alley. Seen only from the front, what a beautiful creature! Noble head! Thick lustrous fur! The dog lay still, with head upraised, surveying the sidewalk with a calm and suffering gaze.

George was afraid to move closer. He didn't know anything about strays. Would it attack? George thought a moment, then set the meat down on the paper bag with a finicky gesture. He walked back to his house and ascended the front steps. After taking out his key and unlocking the door, he hesitated, then locked the door and returned to the alleyway.

The dog still rested. The roast beef, already looking a bit brown, still lay on the paper bag.

"Aren't you hungry, dog? You look hungry."

"I am hungry," the dog said in a deep tone with a piercing glare. "But I will never eat."

Suddenly George understood. The dog would never stop to eat or drink until he found his master.

But he'll probably die, he thought. He'll never find what he's searching for, he'll just keep looking till he drops.

George felt a sob choking him, his throat closing. He clenched his eyes to prevent tears rolling out. The violent pain in his throat and chest surprised him.

All afternoon George wandered the streets, his face raw, his head heavy and confused.

I should be dead, but I'm alive! I gave the roast beef from my sandwich to a stray dog, and he didn't eat it. He didn't eat it!

Ramona Kim had a stomachache today, so departmental affairs had come more or less to a standstill. "Everyone is expendable but my secretary," the Chair was fond of saying. "She runs the place, you know." The deluded Chair thought he was joking.

A tiny smooth woman often obscured by her tall filing cabinets, Ramona in her quiet way commanded steely powers. Other secretaries were mere dithering foot soldiers. Ramona was a four-star general. While her predecessor, Sybil Goldstone, used to disappear into the ladies' forty-five minutes before quitting time to change into mufti and popped incessantly in and out for cigarettes all day long, tireless mysterious Ramona never used the facilities at all.

Ramona said little and moved lightly, humming tuneless snatches, but she was strong in her devotion to the person of the Chair. Not even a full professor, not even a lone gunman, could get into the Chair's private office when Ramona sat guard. When the head of human resources tried to lure her away with promises of long lunch hours and early quits, Ramona not only remained loyal, she reported the attempted seduction.

The Chair sometimes thought Ramona would make him a perfect wife. He hated the thought of Quinton ultimately moving into his office and taking over Ramona.

Because Ramona was feeling dyspeptic today, she didn't take her lunch hour, but gave Gloria, her assistant, extra time to drive over to the mall for some Christmas shopping. Then Dixie from Required Composition, who was scheduled to help while Gloria was out to lunch, didn't show up. Ramona, ill used and out of sorts, was left to command the entire English office, the cramped corral where the secretaries sat, labyrinthine dark corridors leading to high administrative offices, and the mailroom, or, rather, mail closet.

She glided over to Gloria's desk near the entrance, careful not to disturb the huge pile of spring schedules sitting on the desktop. Not much traffic today—a few sleepy students handing in late papers, Igor Blavatsky calling in sick again, a load of blue books delivered by handtruck. Ramona was searching through Gloria's desk drawers for the missing stapler, when a small, well-dressed woman in very high heels came strutting in. Despite dire TV predictions of masses of freezing air from Canada moving into the metropolitan area that very afternoon, the creature was dressed in a long green silk trenchcoat over a short white skirt hardly longer than a dishcloth.

This costume piqued Ramona, who wore Easy Spirit walkers and useful corduroy jumpers to work and who always preferred comfort to glitz. While capable of exquisite courtesy, Ramona was not about to turn it on for someone shorter than herself who had the nerve to wear four-inch heels. "Yes?" she said icily.

"My name is Cynthia Lovitt. I'd like to see the chairman of the department."

"The Chair is unavailable." Ramona eyeballed Cynthia again. "I presume you're a student? Write a memo stating your problem with name, address, telephone number, and student number, and we'll get back to you."

"I'm afraid that won't do," Cynthia said with a toss of her ringletted head. "This is a matter of utmost seriousness."

"In what regard?"

Cynthia bridled, remained silent, looked around the office in search of a better prospect. She turned up her nose at the peeling green filing cabinets, the antique ditto machine. Ramona picked up the spectacles hanging on a chain around her neck, put them on her nose and began leafing through the pile of forms.

"Regarding a complaint," Cynthia said slowly. "Something irregular." Ramona continued to ruffle insolently through the schedules, flip, flip, flip. "Fraud by my English professor."

Ramona didn't twitch. She removed her spectacles. "In that case, I'd advise you to see the associate chair, but he's at the University Senate right now. Why don't you come back tomorrow?"

"You say the associate chair isn't available either. Well, who *is* available?"

Ramona flipped through the metal file box of faculty office hours in elaborate slow motion. "Professor Pryce-Jones."

"Okay, I'll see him."

"HER."

Cynthia screwed up her face. "Who's here tomorrow?"

"The Chair is unavailable. Professor Bloch will be leaving for Dallas. Professor Pryce-Jones is the one you want if you want to complain. Her office is ESF 321. She's in her office now."

As soon as Cynthia flounced out, Ramona was on the phone to Daphne. "Claiming fraud," she said in explanation. "Serious trouble."

"What's her name?"

"Lovitt or Levitt."

"I'll deal with it," Daphne said sternly.

In place of honor on Daphne Pryce-Jones's office wall was a reproduction of a Titian—*Salome with the Head of John the Baptist*, a plump woman carrying part of a green, bearded cadaver. "Wishful thinking," Allen always said.

He was mistaken about her feeling, which was not so much the wish to carry a man's head on a platter, but to be Salome as Titian portrayed her—golden, hefty, and sensual, with rounded uplifted arm, a female cornucopia. Daphne was dark, bony, and waspish with graying fibrous hair like coconut matting shaped in a gladiator's cut and a mouth full of long white teeth.

"You must give her credit for overcoming her looks," Allen once remarked. "Most women with that face would lack confidence, yet somehow Daphne found the strength to become the monster she was born to be." Daphne had blocked Allen's promotion for almost six years.

When Cynthia rushed over to ESF, she didn't know what she was getting into. Her aim—revenge—carried her along on a wave of hyperconfidence. She couldn't have Brian's head, but perhaps she could lose him his job. She didn't care how she damaged him, as long as he was hurt.

Stepping off the elevator, Cynthia flounced down the narrow dim corridor towards Daphne's office, muttering to herself, "I can't believe these English professors. You'd think they were doing something important! Why don't they work nine to five and get real?"

She had never heard of Daphne Pryce-Jones, didn't realize the shoals ahead. She knew only one thing. No man was going to toy with her and then drop her to go back to his wife!

What a way to be dropped! In the parking lot of ESF, headlight beams of departing students rushing across her.

His fat face trying to look concerned and sensitive. "I can't see you anymore, Cynthia. I'm sorry. It's not fair to Tiffany, my wife. I know you'll understand." Did he delude himself into thinking she would be dropped without a squawk? Cynthia rapped with determination on Daphne's door.

Inside she saw a gray-haired wiry woman crouching behind her cluttered desk in an office no bigger than a hatcheck room. "Sit down, Miss Lovitt, and tell me what's on your mind." A little flutter of her dark-lidded eyes showed she didn't think Cynthia would come up with much.

Cynthia lowered herself into the plastic chair, running her ringed hands across her thighs. "I'm a student in Brian McGlinchee's survey course," she said demurely. "Something very troubling happened a couple of weeks ago. I thought the department ought to know."

"Yes?"

"After our class filled out their teacher evaluations, I was supposed to bring them over to the English office. But before I did, he took them from me and changed them."

Daphne unsheathed her steely smile. "Not a very convincing story. Why would he trouble himself?"

"To make himself look better."

"Nonsense."

"Are you telling me you don't believe me?"

"Yes."

"I don't see why you find it so incredible." Cynthia tried without success to outstare Daphne. "But if you don't believe me, maybe the school newspaper will."

"There are libel laws in New York Sate, Miss Lovitt."

"I only describe what's true."

"It's a matter of total indifference to the department what Professor McGlinchee did with those evaluations. If he tampered with them, which I doubt, it wouldn't trouble me. No one pays the slightest attention to them. They're virtually without value."

"It's proof of dishonesty!" Cynthia cried out in shock. She began breathing rapidly.

"We are English faculty, not lawyers or politicians. If I were you, I'd go home and forget about it."

"I'm going to write the chairman and then to the president. After that I'll contact the chancellor."

"You do that, Miss Lovitt. I'm sure the practice will sharpen your writing skills."

"And my name is Mrs. Lovitt. Don't patronize me, you sad little bitch!"

Daphne sprang up. Wedged in as she was in one corner of the tiny cell, she could only draw herself up and snarl, "I'm going to ring the security guard if you don't vacate my office this instant!"

"Very funny. I saw that old geezer in the lobby."

At this moment a barrage of knocks sounded at the door and a frowsy platinum-blond head on meaty shoulders appeared in the door frame. "I heard shouting, Daphne? Do you need any help?"

"Not to worry, Lucille. All is well." Daphne became ever so much more proper whenever vulgar Lucille showed up. "This person is just leaving."

In a flash Cynthia began hyperventilating and fell back, panting, in the student's chair. "Not so fast," she gasped, sipping the air like a fish, the ringlets on her head bobbing up and down. "Not . . . so . . . fast."

"What exactly is her problem? Shall I get a doctor? An ambulance?" Lucille offered. She was a useful tool, Daphne thought, though she showed a bit of softness, if only in the pot belly protruding from her tailored suit or the massive calf peeping through a slit in her long straight skirt. "Campus patrol," replied Daphne. "Pronto."

Cynthia grabbed the sides of her chair and arched her back. "Can't make me . . ."

"Plagiarist?" Lucille asked sotto voce. "Failing grade?"

While outwardly imperturbable, Daphne sensed real danger. Could she protect Brian, her pet, from this neurotic troublemaker? Probably not. A firmly committed crackpot would not be brushed aside by threats. This minimannequin Lovitt had more spirit than one would think from her packaging. Then again, Lovitt was an English name.

"Miss Lovitt has had a trying day." Daphne shoved

her briefcase under the desk with her foot and stepped back to the wall away from her collapsed adversary. "Pity we can't open a window and get her some air. Fresh air, best thing for hysterics."

"Sometimes sleep is helpful, a good night's sleep," Lucille dithered.

"Or a slap."

The door to the corridor remained partly open with Lucille half in and half out. Suddenly Dickie Walter's soigné head and thick spectacles appeared over her shoulder. "Having a caucus?"

Cynthia was instantly calmed by a male voice, her natural audience. Her head rolled. She sniffed and said in a little whisper, "Why won't you believe me? Brian McGlinchee is a dishonest person. He's my lover. I ought to know."

Lucille mooed in outrage, Dickie cackled in glee. Daphne sat back down at her desk and bleated. Now you've torn it, idiot woman. Good-bye, Brian's tenure, good-bye.

Why do I get stuck with all these rotten jobs? Brian asked himself as he scuffed through the dead leaves piled up in the path before him. Anything unpleasant nobody else in the department will do, I do. "Un-pleasant," he muttered, kicking sticks and leaves off the top step while waiting for George to answer the doorbell.

No answer. He rang again. They want me to find the body, I suppose. Couldn't get hold of a relative. Couldn't call the police. Aloud he mocked the Chair's fatuous voice. "Unforeseen consequences. Unfavorable publicity!" A fool's errand. Doing the bidding of fools. Not part of my job description. The Chair had given him an odd look, too, partly searching, partly pitying. Brian leaned on the bell a third time, then thumped loudly on the door with his fist.

"Ahoy, there, George," he called. "Open up!"

Idiot George, you dick! You couldn't have seduced one of the secretaries. Oh, no, it had to be an associate professor. You couldn't have your breakdown quietly. It had to be in a public meeting with the whole school watching. You couldn't do away with yourself during Christmas vacation, oh, no. It had to be the last week of the term. You had to pick my tenure-decision term for your bloody foolery, when I'm at the beck and call of just about anybody.

Brian stamped his feet up and down. It had to be the last week of term when all the papers are due, when they're piling up to the ceiling, when my car is broken down, when every fool in the school wants to see me, when every late essay in the world has found me out. He gave the black enamelled door a light kick, chipping off a few flecks of paint. Liking the hollow sound, he kicked again, wishing he had steel-toed shoes.

Brian had been in a lousy mood ever since regretful-ly saying good-bye to Cynthia. It had been a wrenching farewell, giving up such a sweet luscious creature. No, not the right time for a love affair, not for a man with year-old twins, an exhausted wife, a job in jeopardy. And Cynthia had been growing careless about secrecy. She'd put her hand on his arm in the corridor. She'd called him a few times at home. Luckily, he'd answered. By the way she'd said huskily, "Hel-lo, this is *Sin*-thia," all would be revealed to any listener.

At least he had done the right thing, made a clean break, no lies or hypocrisy. Easy enough just to have acted cool and shitty to Cynthia for a while, provoking quarrels until *she* broke it off. But why be more of a bastard than you had to? Cynthia had been so calm about it, too. She hadn't cried or begged. A real trouper. Her eyes had drooped down in a touching way, as if she wanted to weep, but thought better of it.

The door opened suddenly and Brian stumbled side-ways, grazing his knuckles on the stucco beside the entrance.

"Is that you, McGlinchee?" George said, blinking slowly. "Why are you here?"

Brian found it impossible to shift to the solicitous tone required for his errand. "Ask me in, why don't you?" he said belligerently. "It's freezing out here."

George stared. He was wearing a dingy T-shirt, a pair

of paint-stained chinos, and soiled white crew socks, no shoes. He was less handsome than he used to be, bleary-eyed, gaunt.

"C'mon, let me in." Brian walked over the threshold without further invitation into foul-smelling darkness. From the rustling underfoot he gathered that another pile of crushed leaves lay in the hallway. The place stank of cat piss and mold. Brian felt along the wall and flicked on the light.

He'd never seen such indoor chaos—cyclone-strewn objects lay all over the living room, not just the expected slurry of books and papers, but old paint cans, glass bricks, cartons, wire hangers, sheets of plywood, earth-filled flower pots, pale green pajamas, a sublime combination of storehouse and bomb site. "Were you asleep?"

"Just resting," George said. "I've been trying to clean up, but it's taking a while . . . Why did you come?"

"It wasn't my idea. That god-awful message you left on the departmental answering machine put a flea in the Chair's ear. He sent me to check on you."

"Message?"

"Saying good-bye. You were going west. Your solemn good-bye. Do you remember? This morning?"

Brian recollected the eerie scene in the English office, as the group stood around the desk, playing the message back several times. George's slow halting voice. "I'm going west . . . want to say good-bye and thank you . . .

to all of you. I'm sorry . . . if I gave you . . . trouble. I won't trouble you . . . any longer."

He recalled Ramona's horrified look and the Chair sitting down while they played the message back a few more times. "I'm going west." "But that's slang from the First World War!" Brian objected. "Want to say good-bye. Won't trouble you any longer." It *was* spooky. "And what," Ramona had said, "about all his exams?"

George shook his head, puzzled. He obviously had no memory of any big farewell.

"Are you planning on leaving town, George?" The heat of the apartment was getting to Brian. He peeled off his overcoat, and stood awkwardly clutching it.

"I'm planning to, but not right now." The shaking of George's head was continuing in a way Brian didn't like. "I thought I might go to Tucson," George continued, with those same unnerving pauses, "but not for a while . . . I have a brother there. Haven't seen him . . . recently." There was a longer pause. "This place is . . . starting to get . . . on my nerves."

"I can see that," Brian said, feeling an unwanted surge of pity. "Maybe you'd better go elsewhere."

George gave a little shrug.

"I know you have lots of papers to grade. The Chair wants to know if you anticipate a problem in getting all grades in on time."

George gave another shrug.

"Are you going to get your grades in?" A black insect suddenly buzzed past Brian's head. "What's that? A fly?" It dive-bombed again and he swatted at it. "What's a fly doing here in the middle of winter?"

"'I heard a Fly buzz—when I died,'" George muttered.

"Don't be such a goddamned English teacher!"

"Insects smell carrion." George rubbed his hand across his face. "I know you'll think it odd." George smiled, showing even, still-white teeth. "I apologize for the intrusion, but do you think I can possibly stay at your place tonight? As long as my house is so messy . . . I don't really want to be alone."

Oh, shit, man, don't do this to me, Brian thought. He thought of his two little children, sleeping unprotected in their cribs. What would Tiffany say if he brought home a madman? "Don't you have any relatives in the city?" he asked hopefully.

"Not to speak of. Not live ones."

"Friends?"

"Just my poker group. But I haven't played with them . . . since my bereavement."

Brian looked around for some place to sit down. He draped his coat on a stepladder standing in the middle of the room, then pushed some muddy running shoes off a bridge chair and sat down. His troubles with Cynthia and Tiffany had a sort of normal cast to them now and the massive stack of essays on the buffet at home didn't seem horrible, but vaguely reassuring. He had a car, it sat in the garage, it would run again on Thursday.

"Do you want some Diet Pepsi? That's all I have," George said, stopping his head-shaking for a moment.

"No, thanks."

"Some Chinese noodles?"

"Can you maybe open a window? Or turn off the steam. I'm boiling."

"I'm sorry. The radiator handles got lost somewhere. And the windows are impossible to open. It's a problem." He shrugged.

"They sent me here because they thought you were having a nervous breakdown. That's what it looks like to me."

George shook his head in the other direction. "Yes, it appears so."

Brian thought for a moment about tangled connections to the world. "Do you have your brother's telephone number. I'd like to talk to him. If you'll let me help you, I think we might get you to Tucson this very night."

On Monday the Chair, Quinton, Dickie, and Daphne held a quick powwow about Brian's fate. They didn't bother to convene a formal P & B meeting, but gathered in Quinton's office with the door locked. Less room than in the Chair's office, but at least it was soundproof.

Daphne and Dickie didn't trouble to carry in chairs, but powwowed standing up.

"I don't know what to do," the Chair said morosely. "It looks bad for Brian, but nothing may happen. There's been such a monster fuss lately about faculty-student relationships. I just don't know."

"He took care of George very neatly," Daphne reminded. "A job well done."

"It's a powder keg with this vindictive female on the loose." Quinton shook his head. "Best to play safe and get rid of Brian. Or, better, defer his tenure decision 'for budgetary reasons.'"

All heads shook sadly at Brian's fall.

"You know, we can simplify everything by just rehiring Cherry," said the Chair. "She *is* the best qualified. It would save union turmoil."

"Over my dead body," countered Quinton. "She really gave it to me after the last department meeting. Walked up to me and emptied both barrels. Called me an assassin for not supporting her, a sneaky double-dealer! Very unattractive, a vindictive female. A wound in the side of the department. I'd rather lose the funding altogether than rehire Cherry."

"Let's just hire someone from the outside," Daphne suggested. "Cool the flames a bit."

"I know!" Dickie cried. "I have a friend at U Conn who's desperate to move to New York. He has twice the publications Brian has. His work on Sir Philip Sidney is spectacular."

"We need someone cheap."

"Oh, he'd be cheap. A single man, simple tastes, but he has a problem about driving that makes his life in suburbia untenable. Mind you, don't misunderstand, the sanest man you can meet, not in the same category as George Reilly, just a minor phobia."

Daphne brightened as much as was possible for her. "Why must we make an immediate decision? Let's bring your chap and some others in for interviews, stretch it out as long as possible. Then if Brian seems trouble free, we can just forget about 'em."

The Chair gave a small, self-contained groan. "Daphne, do keep in mind what all this hiring entails. Once we go the interview route, not only do we have to set up many appointments, two or three days completely shot, barely able to lift our heads from the pillow, we'll also have to comply with affirmative action or we'll get the university officer down on our head. Think about it—filing our search plan, then all those ads—*Black Issues, La Prensa, Korean Times, Oggi*. All that work for nothing."

"If I may bring a *bit* of reality into the scenario," Quinton put in. "Why interview for Renaissance, when only one line may be available and we need someone to teach modern poetry?"

The Chair said, "Dear me," and Dickie frowned.

"We can interview for both." Daphne grew brisk with happiness. "The same ad—same search plan—won't cost a penny extra!"

"Seems like a good idea," Dickie agreed, leaning negligently against a filing cabinet and unwrapping a Mars bar.

"Okay, let's do that," said Quinton.

"I'm glad we can reach a consensus so easily. Good group we have, eh?" The Chair chuckled. "Though some work is involved here, I hope you understand. Who's going to speak to Brian?"

Silence.

"He ought to know what's going on."

"I'll do it," said Daphne reluctantly.

Brian already had the idea something was wrong. No one would sit next to him in the faculty lunchroom, the first clue. Dickie skittered off with his tray to the garbage disposal instead of lingering to chat. Quinton ran out of the men's room when he entered. The mystery deepened with a note in his mailbox. "See me immediately. DPJ" written in a black stabbing hand. Puzzled, Brian dashed over to ESF and up three flights of stairs. Daphne was just locking her office door to go home for the day. She motioned him inside.

Daphne wasn't used to giving sympathy. As a young teacher, her favorite writing exercise for freshmen was something called "Who's to Blame?" Students pondered a complicated domestic disaster, then wrote a five-hundred-word essay on whose fault it was—jealous father, indifferent wife, careless boyfriend, self-pitying daughter. No problem fulfilling the word limit here, with so many characters to blame. Daphne herself composed a model essay full of endless recriminations.

Now she motioned Brian to sit in the plastic chair. He was looking older, thinner, less fresh-faced and ruddy. Her rundown of the situation was brief and pitiless.

"So, you see, Brian, this Cynthia person at this moment may be denouncing you to the president. Or maybe not. Who knows? Forewarned is forearmed, however. If the president's office is going to veto you for fraternization and fraud, there's no point in our proposing you."

Speechless, Brian put his head in his hands and leaned his elbows heavily on Daphne's desk. Inside his head was a bleak vision of a little community college in New Jersey or the Bronx, someplace worse than Muni where *all* the students chewed gum. Or cast out in the countryside in some hick town without a bakery or sidewalks, or going door to slamming door. And there was Tiffany, reminding him of his marriage proposal when he promised tenure and solvency. And how, before the vasectomy, he hadn't wanted to use birth control, he'd wanted sons. He lowered his head to the desk.

Daphne stared down at the head lying on her blotter. During her long career Daphne had seen several students in exactly this pose, but never before a colleague and protégé. She had a sudden desire to bend down and sink her teeth into the meaty neck.

"After all your hard work, you've really mucked this one up, haven't you?" With her elegant British diction Daphne sounded as if she were discussing some delicate point of etiquette. "Can't you persuade Miss Lovitt to silence? Promise her something nice? A trip to Aspen?"

Brian silently shook his head, pressing his forehead against the stiff leather edge of the blotter.

Daphne's hand lingered above his sweat-soaked hair. "You've been very naughty. What possessed you? Oh, well, some questions are best not asked. It's embarrassing to me, too, you know, because I fought for you quite single-mindedly."

For a moment Brian seemed to shudder inside his tweed jacket. "I'm really sorry, Daphne," he muttered in a phlegm-filled voice.

"Meanwhile, we'll be interviewing to fill Lauren's line. You'd be astonished at how many people want that line. Hundreds, most of them completely unsuitable. Meanwhile, you'll do well to put out feelers elsewhere. I wouldn't buy a house or take out a mortgage, if I were you. Are you quite sure you can't silence this person?"

Brian looked up. "With a gun maybe."

"Well, don't do that!" Daphne cried archly. "Avoid bloodshed at any cost. My invention is failing, or I'd think of a way out for you."

"You don't *own* a gun, do you?"

"Stop thinking about weapons and start thinking of expedients." She gave what was for Daphne a very supportive gesture. She patted him twice on the shoulder with one brown-speckled paw, a slight twist of humor in her bony mouth, the shadow of a smile.

On the way home from work, Brian stopped at the T-Bone Diner. It wasn't a favorite place, or even a decent place, just a spot near home where he could get a drink and still be back in time to pick up Tiffany for her Mothers of Twins meeting.

He chose a booth in the very back near the men's room and the telephone. Quiet and smelly. Just what he wanted.

"I'll have a double vodka martini," he told the Greek farm boy in waiter's uniform. Then he sat picking the paper napkin apart. He'd brought along his accordion-pleated file folder, intending to work on programs, but he didn't have the heart for administrative work after listening to Daphne's news.

The suspense—not knowing whether he was ruined—that's what would wreck him. As he sipped his martini, he flipped through the programs in his folder.

Not a single teacher in the department was satisfied with his teaching schedule. Everyone wanted changes. El-Okdah had a long-standing tennis appointment on Tuesday and Thursday mornings. Burnson had a weekly doctor's appointment that looked suspiciously like a shrink, or maybe it was a methadone treatment. Blavatsky, the part-timer, had two other part-time jobs, one in Philadelphia. "I'll give them changes," Brian muttered to himself, changing his sipping to gulping.

When he felt squished enough, he made up his mind to call Cynthia. That's why he'd sat near the telephone, he decided.

Cynthia's voice had altered completely, grown coarse with a touch of Brooklyn. "Why are you calling me?" she demanded.

"Why call? I don't know. I can't stand not knowing, I guess."

Cynthia cackled like some crazy fishwife. "Come to the point. I'm busy."

"Why are you ruining me? Why did you talk to Professor Pryce-Jones? Have some pity, Cynthia."

"Are you drunk? Your voice sounds sappier than usual."

"Why are you so nasty?"

"This isn't a very interesting conversation. Why don't you hang up and go back to Tiffany?"

"I'm not even sure why you're doing this. Do you want to get married? Is that it?"

"You must be joking. I hope I never see you again. I've met someone far superior to you, an advertising executive, a fellow with brains, money, and charm, not a dickhead like you, Brian."

"What will you do about your complaint to the college?"

"I'll do what I feel like doing."

He let the receiver dangle as he made a sudden nauseated dash for the men's room. Her jeering voice followed him. "You're not a real man, Brian, just a lousy jerkoff."

In his heart Brian agreed, for when he fled the T-Bone Diner, he left his folder with programs for the whole English department on the floor below the telephone.

5

The first interruption came just as Steve was getting down to the most fascinating research, sitting at his kitchen table, sifting through photocopied diaries. With satisfaction he lined up all the index cards headed WAR. "Alistair Byrd reported visiting Henry Martin at his home in Holland Park in 1914 and being repelled by his views against the war," he wrote, smiling faintly. "He accused him of being a German sympathizer." Then he heard the downstairs buzzer rasping.

Who could it be? Aimee was in Switzerland with her folks for two weeks. Paranoid fantasies began swarming through his brain. The FBI—that petition to reopen the Rosenberg case? His mother's new husband come to even the score?

"Who is it?"

A sweet, serious young woman's voice. "My name is Dawn Kallison, and I'd like to talk to you about the origin of life."

Shocked, Steve did nothing. He mulled it over, coming up with more paranoid fantasies. The police posing as a pretty woman? The IRS? But they owed *him* money. When he finally did push the buzzer to open the downstairs door, there was no reply. Had Dawn changed her mind? Or been hit over the head and raped while waiting for him to respond?

Cautiously he opened the front door, advanced into the grimy hallway and peered over the decaying banister. No screams or whimpers. No tramping feet. Nothing. He went back inside, police-locked the door, then walked through the whole apartment to the front window and peered down at the sidewalk. Nothing, unless you counted the ceaseless flow of human traffic, black, white, and yellow, as nothing. A blue-rinsed old lady with a miniature schnauzer. A skinny youth in cerise bicycle shorts puffing whitened breaths. A transvestite in pastel drag, blonde wig, yellow sunglasses, and earmuffs. If I move out of the city to get a job, I'll miss this scene, he thought. Is that good or bad?

The ringing telephone brought him scrambling back through the apartment to the kitchen.

He heard Allen's pleasant, slightly nasal voice, an unpleasant interruption like the buzzing of a nest of wasps.

"Good news for you, Steve. The P & B is now actively interviewing for Lauren's line. Why, I have no idea, but this gives you a chance to put yourself forward. I'm sure they'd prefer a department member to an outsider. My guess is that they want someone really cheap at the assistant professor level."

Steve focused his mind with some difficulty. "How many lines do they have to fill?"

"Haven't a clue, but that's irrelevant. Ask Ramona for an application right away. They have this nutty form to fill out, Daphne's idea. It would be better if they'd invited you, but . . . You haven't any new publications?"

"No."

"That would be helpful."

"All this committee work is cutting down on my research time." Steve tried not to sound aggrieved. "I now arrive on campus at ten in the morning and remain till ten at night, turning up punctually at department meetings, lectures, prize award ceremonies, committee meetings, trying always to present a neat alert appearance which, believe me, is not easy."

"You didn't become an academic for instant gratification. Listen, I've got cheap group tickets for a *Hamlet* matinee on the twenty-third. Would you be interested?"

"Oh. Sounds good. But I have to ask my girlfriend if we're doing anything. She's out of town."

"Oh." Did Allen sound disappointed? "Well, tell me if you need a ticket. We could have a bite afterward."

Steve hated to approach Ramona for anything. She

always gave him an intimidating stare which he read as "Who's this? A member of the department? Looks more like someone who sleeps in a cardboard box. Did we really hire this disreputable character?" But all she ever uttered was a chilling "Yes?"

"I understand you're interviewing for an assistant professorship. I'd like to put in my own application."

Ramona silently opened a drawer. She pulled out a form, but it certainly wasn't the application because she put it face down on her desk.

To Steve's dismay, Daphne's wraithlike form stepped out of the mailroom at this moment and stood watching the scene.

"So, shall I fill it out?"

"The application?"

"I want to apply."

"By all means," Ramona said, reexamining the paper and handing it over. She turned to give Daphne a significant look.

Steve felt a wave of humiliation sweep over him. They didn't even want him to *apply* for the job. "Any deadline?" he asked in a numb voice.

"Monday. Absolutely not one day later," Daphne put in from the doorway. Did she recognize him? "Later is out of the question."

Steve took the form home. He bought a new typewriter ribbon and filled out the application meticulously after looking up the dates of all his articles again and rechecking his references. He returned it to Ramona early Monday morning, then heard nothing further about the job, no acknowledgment, no request for additional materials, no request for an interview. Nothing. To him the process seemed more mysterious than the origin of life.

Even Allen was puzzled. "Did you tell Ramona you were applying?"

"Of course. How else would I get the application? And what do I need an application for, anyway? Every place else you just write a letter. Why do we always have to do things the half-assed way?"

Allen shrugged. "Ramona may simply be holding on to it."

"What for?"

"Who knows."

"She's only the departmental secretary for godsakes. This job is more trouble than it's worth," he said petulantly.

"Really, now." Allen fixed him with a quizzical look. "Don't you think it's worth a little effort on your part? Don't you ever work and suffer for a goal, a highly desirable goal?"

"Is being an assistant professor at Muni a highly desirable goal?"

Allen laughed. "Such an innocent. I can't believe it. I'll speak to my ear on the P & B and try to find out about your application, but I can't promise success. You have to be more motivated, Steve, or your career is over. I hope I don't see you out on the sidewalk one day with your bundles of notecards."

"That's not very nice," Steve said, but Allen kept laughing.

Jane, a short, dour-looking woman with plain expressionless features, silently entered Allen Swain's cubicle where he lay naked under a coarse white sheet. "Good afternoon," she said curtly, then began preparing her materials at her table without uttering another word.

At almost the same moment in the next cubicle, a tiny young woman in a spotless white uniform approached Quinton Bloch. "I'm May. Debbie no longer work here."

"Too bad. She had nice delicate fingers. Try to imitate her style. I like a light touch."

"I have light touch."

Next door, Jane, smiling sourly to herself, uncovered Allen's tanned back and shoulders and began rubbing scented oil between her palms. She transferred the warmed oil to Allen's back and massaged vigorously, keeping one hand firmly on his skin while she added more oil.

"Umm, feels good."

"Just the way I like it," Quinton declared as May's

flitting fingers caressed his massive shoulders lightly, ever so lightly. "Good . . . good."

"How did you find out about this place, anyway?" Quinton tried to project his voice over the partition towards Allen. It was hard because his face kept sinking forward.

"Through the card in my mailbox, same as you. One complimentary visit to Seoul Healing Arts."

"Oh, I didn't realize the whole department got cards . . . I thought one of my students . . ."

"We all did. I've been wondering, though. Who put them in?"

Silence. Both men had the same idea simultaneously—could it have been Ramona?—but neither voiced his suspicion.

The ear on the P & B Committee that Allen Swain had referred to so mysteriously was indeed the thick, fleshy organ of Quinton Bloch. Since both men were creatures of habit, they regularly bumped into each other on Thursday afternoons when they went to unwind at Seoul Healing Arts after the rigors of their two-day work week. A few minutes of departmental chitchat livened their routine.

"Aaah," said Quinton as May's skillful hands moved down over his buttocks and thighs. "The kinks are coming out, all right."

"Do you know who'll replace you if you go to

NYU?" Allen asked as casually as possible. To interrogate as a disembodied voice took all Addison DeWitt's skill.

"One of the other Aaam . . . American lit people will take over for the time being." Quinton's voice was thick.

"And the line?" Allen relentlessly pursued.

"Oh, oh, oh, the line," Quinton gasped. "Still un, uhn, clear."

"You're still, you're still interviewing for Lauren's line?"

"Yes . . . yes," Quinton breathed. "Umm . . . yes."

"Any idea why Steve Speck hasn't been called for an interview?"

No answer for a long time. "Turn, please," said May.

"No idea, none," Quinton declared suddenly in a stronger and grumpier voice, as he moved his bulk. "How should I know? What do you care, anyway?"

"Just because . . . I have a . . ." Allen's voice sank away. He exhaled. "Curiosity only."

"Turn over, please," said Jane.

Then all conversation came to an end as each man communed with himself alone.

Finally, the summons came. Among the papers stuffed in Steve's mailbox, the well-known white departmental envelope with the orange-and-green seal of the Beaver and the Windmill. "The P & B Committee will see you in the Chair's office at 4 P.M. on Monday."

Steve's stomach lurched. He hadn't really been paying attention. He hadn't thought it through, interrogation by those familiar, far-from-Olympian figures. What unanswerable questions would the P & B come up with? What opportunities for humiliation? What traps? Soon his disquiet gave way to despair. What chance did he have, really, of getting a desirable line? Why would they take him? There were so many other talented people.

When Steve made his weekly telephone call to his mother in San Francisco, for want of other news he told her about his forthcoming interview. Well, perhaps he wished her to know that he had at least a chance of advancement, so she'd be proud of him. She was.

"That's wonderful news, dear. Good luck and all that," she said.

"But I don't think I'll get it."

"No?"

"Maybe they already have someone else lined up. That often happens, I'm told."

"Someone more qualified than you?" she went on in an unbelieving voice. "A brilliant student?" (As a schoolboy, Steve had been called Straight-A Speck.)

"Maybe. I'm qualified, I admit it. But I haven't had that much teaching experience. Not that they pay any attention to teaching. Okay, from the teaching and research point of view, I'm highly qualified. But I'm sort of an outsider here, so I feel pretty worthless on that score."

"*Worthless*?" His mother pounced on the word. "Why should that be? You were always treated like a little prince all through childhood. Why would you feel worthless? You always got the best of care and attention. A young rajah!"

Steve sought to calm her. "Of course I got good care at home. But that doesn't cover the outside world. You get bad treatment outside the family, and it makes you feel like shit."

"Oh, dear." Now she really sounded upset. "You should have told me. You should feel good about yourself. I know that. I would have done something."

"Not to worry, Ma. I do feel good about the interview. Actually very calm. Optimistic. I'll be fine."

"What are you going to wear? Will you let Aimee pick out your outfit?" His mother sounded wistful. "Promise me, please, you won't wear that green shirt, you know, the one you wore out here the last few times."

Steve was sorry he had ever mentioned the interview. Aimee was still in Switzerland with her parents, but he wasn't going to tell his mother. What if she flew out to dress him? "Don't worry, I'll be neat but devastating. Don't give it a thought."

"Don't forget to let me know how it goes."

"Sure. But they won't give me an answer for quite a while. I know this English department. Maybe not for weeks. Maybe never."

On Sunday night Steve had trouble falling asleep. He kept hearing voices of the P & B Committee, the Chair's suave oratory, Quinton's solid bark like the hound after the fox, Dickie's simper, Daphne's bite, Lucille's vacuous laugh. As these sounds rose and fell in his ears, Steve suddenly felt rage. He grappled with it, turning uneasily in his bed.

He had contempt for them, for their petty meanness, their self-satisfied airs. To submit to their judgment was galling. He was more talented than they were, as a scholar and as a human being. That was the crux. They were contemptible, but they had the power. How could he put on a smooth submissive face and smile through this interview?

He began tossing wildly, beating his pillow with his fists. If only Aimee were here. But he was alone with his fury. This is intolerable. Forget about it. Less than dust beneath their feet. He hated the bastards. Then Steve remembered Allen's words in the doughnut shop. "If you're difficult or brilliant, they'll cast you out."

Since it was impossible for Steve to regard himself for long as either difficult or brilliant, within seconds his anger died. He went back to feeling depressed. He stopped tossing, and after a short masturbatory interlude, fell asleep.

At four P.M. on Monday Steve was standing humbly

at the rail in the English department office, watching Gloria file reports on English majors. She stared at him.

"They're way behind. Started interviewing late. I guess I should have called you in ESF so you could wait in your office."

"Guess so."

"Why don't you get a chair and sit in the hallway? The interviewee before you is still waiting out there."

As he transported his chair, Steve felt chilled, unreal, as if he were having an out-of-body experience. In other departmental offices he'd glimpsed comfortable sofas or easy chairs. In other departments he'd even seen good-looking, smiling secretaries. The chill spread to his fingers and toes.

Ridiculous. He'd had plenty of interviews, in college, grad school, in this very same office two years ago. But never before had he felt whipped before he'd begun. What was it about this place?

Sitting on a straight-backed chair in the corridor was a fellow only a little older than Steve, but much more tastefully dressed, in a dark blue shirt, silk rep tie, and heathery gray tweed jacket with leather patches. He grinned at Steve.

Steve set his chair down at a companionable distance. "Hello, how's it going?"

"Been waiting nearly an hour. This is my fourth interview in two days. I scheduled them too close together, and boy, am I reeling!" The young man glanced down the dark corridor towards the Chair's office. "I think they're grilling them in there." He shifted impatiently in his chair. "This place is sort of dingy, isn't it?" he said in a lower tone. "Reminds me of a rundown high school."

Steve was staring obsessively at his fellow interviewee, thinking, why would they take me, when they could have a high-powered guy with patches? "I know," he replied. "I've worked here two years and I'm still surprised at how shabby everything is."

His companion drew back and gazed at him speculatively. "Oh, so you know the setup. Tell me, can I get an Internet account?"

Steve looked at him blankly.

"Yeah, I want to send some e-mail to my buddy at Berkeley. What do you use?"

"I use note topic slips and work in the library," said Steve, feeling more and more like an unemployable drudge. "Sometimes I get photocopies mailed from London from a friend of my mother."

"In 1985 they don't have e-mail?"

"Maybe you don't understand the situation here. We've had about twenty years of budget cuts, and everything, just everything, is outmoded." He mimed total idiocy. "If we want copies, we have to cut a ditto!"

"No point asking about PCs then. I guess I'd just bring in my laptop. But you know, I really want to be in

California. If Berkeley falls through, I'd consider the East Coast, but I'm really not planning to be here. With all due respect, looks like a dead end."

"Some excellent people here, though," Steve found himself saying. "Depends what you want."

The door to the Chair's office opened and a stunning Indian woman in a sari walked back past them toward the English office. Lucille followed.

"Mr. Hargroves?" she said, looking straight at Steve.

"That's me," said the young guy. "Best of luck!" He nodded at Steve. "First-world males don't stand a chance here, I bet," he whispered, then followed Lucille back down the corridor. In less than fifteen minutes he was out again. Walking past Steve, he crossed his eyes and stuck out his tongue.

"Dr. Speck," Quinton was calling.

As Steve stumbled up the shadowy corridor toward the Chair's office, he thought he heard a scornful "Worse than I thought" from Daphne, or was it a "Where has he taught?"

In the Chair's sunlit double office only Quinton stood to shake his hand. "I'm sure you've all met Dr. Speck," he said.

The prisoner will step before the bar. Nods all around, as Steve seated himself in a rickety office chair whose plastic spine wobbled. The rest of the committee sat in inquisitorial splendor in a half-circle, the Chair behind his wooden desk the centerpiece, rumpled, tired, querulous; Lucille, big white pudding, half-asleep; Dickie, sharp, enjoying himself. Daphne had a clipboard as well as a fat file folder. She greeted him with a vulpine gleam of teeth.

On the desk in front of the Chair sat a large old open-reel Webcor tape recorder, identical to the one Steve's father had thrown away when he was a little boy. He remembered lying submissively on the scratchy carpet in front of it while it played ghostly messages from his grandparents.

"Recent developments have led us to record all interviews," Quinton explained. "I'm sure you won't mind."

Steve shook his head no.

Lucille leaned forward.

"Press forward and record, both," Quinton cautioned her. "And it's best if you say yes or no, Dr. Speck, instead of nodding."

As if in a dream they led Steve through his graduate school experience. His thesis advisor, Desmond Delius, a notorious lecher whom Steve detested, was an old buddy of the Chair. Delius had obstructed Steve's progress for several years, then let him off easy while Delius was going through his fourth messy divorce. "Yes, working for Delius was quite an experience," Steve said sincerely, choosing his words with care. "He didn't let me get away with much, heh heh heh."

"Heheheh," they all echoed. "Heheheh."

"And you're currently working on a book?"

"Yes, a critical biography of Henry Martin." Steve remembered to hold his head high, to enunciate clearly.

Lucille opened her eyes wide. "Didn't he have an affair with Anaïs Nin?"

"No, that was somebody else entirely," Steve replied. "Henry Miller."

"Henry Martin? Frankly, never heard of him." Dickie seemed amused.

"Fascinating figure," Steve explained, unclenching his fists. Why did it sound as if he were faking his enthusiasm? "Son of a draper, lower middle class, eccentric. Really did his own thing all the way. Triple First at Oxford. Spent the years after World War I as head gardener on Lord Rondmere's estate. Never married."

"Head gardener?" The Chair's ears pricked up. "Do you know what his specialty was?"

"As a matter of fact, I do, because gardening is about the only thing he mentions in his postwar letters, never discusses poetics, or his personal life, not at all. My guess is that he had some sort of tragic loss during the war, since he never mentions that time. I'm eager to explore his war years."

"Or nothing happened," Daphne said drily. "One good reason not to mention it—nothing happened, nothing to mention. When I was a girl in England, Martin was considered a popular poet—now best forgotten. Louis

MacNeice made fun of him, if you remember, in 'Some Garden Pomposities.'"

"That canard has been exploded!" Steve tried to sound respectful, though his heart was full of hate. "MacNeice undoubtedly meant Linus Tate as a target, not Martin. See Forbush's internal evidence in *Hound and Horn*, August 1954."

"Wouldn't your time be more profitably spent on a less minor figure?" Dickie asked in a mock-helpful tone. "You don't have a contract for the book yet, do you?"

"What is minor, after all?" Steve replied judiciously, suppressing the geyser of rage that threatened to spew out of him. "He exemplifies all that's basic in English society. Because his subjects are homely, doesn't that make him more, not less, relevant to the scene?"

"Our field is literature, not sociology," Quinton remarked with a little twitch of his big moustache.

"But you never told us what Martin's garden specialties were," the Chair demanded. "You've avoided mentioning them. Lilies, for example? What did he say about lilies?"

"He considered them too easy and too showy," Steve went on in a strong voice, some of his confidence returning. He'd held his own so far, he thought. "'Hush the lily, too quick to please' says it all. And in *The Quiet Kitchen Garden*, 'the overweening pride of lilies, faith stripped of spiritual joy,' circa 1922."

"Humph," said the Chair.

"What he liked was the slow growth and difficult propagation of heathers. Heathers were his specialty." Steve was winging it here, uncertain of his ground, but who on earth would be able to refute him? He had the only New York copy of Martin's garden diaries on his bureau at home. "Also ladyfern—'ornamental yet unassuming frond' was another enthusiasm to which he devoted two lyrics and a mention in *Lament for George Babbington Taylor*." He opened his mouth as if to quote, but the Chair got there first.

"As to your limited teaching experience," he broke in, now unaccountably in a stern adversarial tone, "is it really adequate to support a professorial line?"

"If you look at my observation reports in your files, you'll see that they're all rated satisfactory. And my student evaluations were excellent."

The Chair shuffled through a crackling mass of onionskin. "Looking at your English 1 grade sheets, I discover that you've only failed one student since you began teaching at Muni. Your standards don't seem very high."

Steve hadn't expected this one. He hesitated, then went on. "I work my composition students very hard, one essay a week, and I go over each failing paper with the student until it passes. So, if they don't drop out and manage to make it to the end of the term—I pass 'em."

"You pass 'em?"

"Extraordinary," Daphne said. "But we don't expect you to pass all your students. Irregular, very. Failure is also a teaching tool."

Dickie shook his head dismissively. "You haven't taught a single literature class since you've been here, so you can't expect us to judge your abilities—the requisite for *this* position."

"I haven't been *assigned* any literature classes," Steve retorted in a muffled voice. "But I'm sure I would have acquitted myself just as well if I had—*maybe better*!" he burst out against his own will.

"Yes, yes." Dickie rolled his eyes upward.

Oh, that's so insulting, Steve thought. I'd like to kick his ass.

"Time is getting on. Let's have one last question." Quinton said. "You, Lucille?"

Lucille smiled. "We all know you have an unorthodox style of doing things. Unorthodoxy doesn't trouble *me*, but . . ." She closed her eyes to enigmatic slits. Was she talking about baby-sitting or going over student papers till they passed?

"Tell me, Mr. Speck, why do you wish to continue teaching *here*?"

Oh, shit. Steve mentally crossed all his fingers and toes. "Why, I'm very happy and satisfied here. Good atmosphere, fine students. I can visualize teaching here for the rest of my life."

Till I kill myself, he added. In a pig's eye, everyone's face said. Hogwash.

"I feel we've had ample opportunities to glean information from you. We thank you very much for coming in to talk with us," Quinton added, since the Chair showed no sign of speech but kept looking reproachfully at his Rolex Oyster. "Before you go, perhaps you have a last question for us?"

How much will you pay me? flashed through Steve's head. Instead he asked, "When do you think you'll come to a decision?"

Ooh. Taboo question. "Situation fluid. Other factors. Can't say at the moment." They were still mumbling about budgetary considerations as they turned off the circling Webcor and showed him the door.

Steve prepared himself for being fired. Allen's early words about endangering his job now came back to haunt him. In the past few weeks he'd refined his natural aptitude for worry, dismissing his father's old steadying aphorism, "You can't fall out of bed when you're sleeping on the floor." He still had his job, so he wasn't on the floor—yet.

All the little economies he'd been practicing—never under any circumstances hailing a taxi, forcing himself to pull his shirts out of the dryer on time instead of using the Chinese laundry, wearing his undershirts till you could read the *New York Times* through them—these counted little without a paycheck to practice on.

When Aimee returned from Switzerland and he confessed his fears, she pooh-poohed his worries. "You're too bright and dedicated a teacher to be fired. Even if they do screw you, I'm sure you can get a better job somewhere else. Municipal College isn't that great, anyway, and besides, I can pay the full rent for a while."

At the moment Aimee was taking a course in decoupage at the School of Visual Arts and learning bookbinding at the Fine Arts Book Center. Her parents had just increased her allowance, some big stock tender windfall in her trust fund, and after two weeks at a Swiss spa she enjoyed the transcendent pure beauty of a twenty-year-old. Hell, she was a twenty-year-old, and what did she know about academic promotion?

Steve kissed the tanned luscious neck arising from the butternut cashmere sweater. Aimee's thick dark hair bounced on her shoulders, and the purple shadows under her eyes had all but disappeared. Steve's tigress was turning into a tabby cat.

The imbalance in their budget was getting to him, though. His two-dollar Giant Economy shampoo stood on the bathtub shelf next to her tiny purple bottle of Diffusion de Chamomille and Apple Blossom. Aimee's suppers of rare pumpernickels, imported chèvres, and someone else's home-cooked ravioli from Zabar's were delicious, but they preyed on Steve in his penny-watching mood.

Once Aimee threw away a brown paper bag full of five-cent Bud cans he'd been saving to take back to the deli. "Because they were in my way!" she pouted. "And I kept knocking them over. Who needs the stupid things!"

How could he explain how demoralizing that gesture was?

He lay rigidly in his Salvation Army bedstead now covered with teal satin sheets. Aimee flung herself in beside him, unbuttoned his pajama top and kissed his smooth chest. "Why should they fire you? Give me one reason. When we're so happy, why must you worry?"

"Because they hate me. Lucille Streng is out to get me. The way she acted at the interview. I behaved well, but she pretended I'm a lunatic. When my contract runs out, they won't renew. They have a budget crisis. They're going to fire everyone!"

Steve continued his insomniac nights. He felt jumpy even though he'd stopped drinking coffee. His handwriting on his notes was now almost illegible.

One morning he finally got himself in shape for work, the labor he wanted to do, enjoyed doing. While he was sorting through a pack of notes labeled Martin's Trip to Tintagel, his mind lucid and relaxed and miles away from Muni College budget cuts and the protests to the governor in Albany and pep sessions called by the union, the telephone rang. He heard with a flash of terror the unctuous voice asking for "Dr. Speck." Now it's coming.

"Speck speaking."

"Quinton Bloch, here. We're changing your course load."

"I've got the line?"

"No, no." Quinton chuckled. "We're far from coming to a decision on *that*. We have a staffing emergency. You're down for two freshman comps and one remedial, but Professor Reilly is now on disability leave, and we're having problems filling his electives. You see, *he* was taking over from Professor Bjornsen, who is also on disability, and the way the sabbaticals are working out . . . Would you be able to take the Joyce seminar on short notice?"

"The *James* Joyce seminar?"

"Yes, of course."

"I would. I'd be delighted."

Silently Steve danced around the kitchen table, lifting his long legs high and throwing his blank index cards in the air.

"A slight schedule change. The Joyce will meet at 9:10 Tuesdays and Thursdays."

Steve, who saw himself as Dedalus, suddenly heard the seagulls on the Liffey and caught a glimpse of the girl on the strand in the likeness of a beautiful seabird, a more ethereal creature than Aimee. "To live, to err, to fall, to triumph . . ." Not that he knew anything much about Joyce.

How will I be able to prepare this course in two weeks? Steve asked himself and stopped capering. I've only read Joyce through once, don't know beans about him. A complex modern writer takes years to explore.

"Enrollment should be very high," Quinton added, "since we had to cut some other electives. Expect a crowd."

"First we feel, then we fail, then we fall." Rows of eager heads, arms scrabbling to keep up with the furious pace of his lecture. Little gems from Leon Millman, his grad school teacher, a real Joyce scholar, interspersed with his own rare musings, his photo of Number 7 Eccles Street. He'd manage.

"Glad it's working out," said Quinton. "I was afraid we'd have to get someone from comp lit. I'll have Ramona send you the book lists. They're overdue, so don't delay, or the bookstore will have puppies. Also, remember to check the prerequisites of every student in the room. Unqualified rascals always try to sneak in where they don't belong."

After two grueling weeks on Joyce's trail, Steve felt less exhilarated. At the Mordecai Raskin Memorial Library on campus, near the checkout turnstile, a high-tech frisking device, he ran into Allen, his short arms loaded with videocassettes, *The Cabinet of Dr. Caligari* on top.

"Well done!" Allen said effusively. "I saw the class schedule. You engineered a coup with this Joyce seminar. Congratulations!"

"I didn't engineer anything," Steve replied. "They just called out of the blue and offered it to me. Looking for a warm body."

"But why *your* warm body? No, Steve, it's a coup of sorts. They're taking you seriously."

"Oh, sure."

"Don't you want to be taken seriously?"

"Mmm. Yeah."

"You're a difficult person to congratulate."

"But why—" Steve said, turning to Allen passionately and nearly knocking him over—"isn't it a course I'm qualified to teach? Pound? Eliot? Auden? Something like that. That would make me think they had *me* in mind, Steve Speck, *my* qualifications."

"You want life to be perfectly rational? Be thankful you're remembered."

"I'm thankful. I *am* thankful. I'm just also dissatisfied."

"With?"

"The way they do things around here. How deeds and rewards don't add up. How skewed it is—the haves and the have-nots."

"You want to be a *have-not*?"

"No! Dammit! I'd just like to feel more in control of my destiny."

"Oh, man!" Allen said. "*Schwere Neurotiker*!"

6

The second semester began with the usual madness of the first day of school complicated by a medium-grade snow-storm. Faculty divided into two groups—those who had made heroic efforts to show up despite poor snow removal and those who didn't bother. Igor Blavatsky made the most stunning effort by walking from Brooklyn. When he appeared red-faced with white patches on his forehead below his fur hat, he was greeted with excitement in the English office for a minute or two. "Good work," they called as he exited. "Didn't think that fuckup would put himself out," said Ramona. "Gloria couldn't make it from ten blocks away."

Quinton, associate chair, had the worst headaches. "The chancellor couldn't declare a snow day? What's the problem?"

The Chair shook his head. "We've got the state on our backs. Don't forget we took two flood and hurricane days in the fall."

Requests for section changes, overtallies to grossly overcrowded classrooms, missing instructors, erroneous class schedules, duplicated room assignments—all these problems and more poured into the English office.

Ramona's pet peeve was foreign students who couldn't speak English flocking to her desk. They'd failed the proficiency exam, were assigned to remedial classes, then couldn't find the classrooms. They made large gestures with melodramatic asides in broken English, cluttering up her office. Then there were those native speakers who'd also failed the proficiency exam and were trying desperately to avert the stern decree. Quinton took no prisoners as far as these lunkheads were concerned, but they were surprisingly resourceful in their ploys to skip remedial work. At the registration desk, he'd had to lock up the exemption-permission slips in a metal cashbox to avoid pilferage.

"Chaos is normal here," Quinton told the Chair. "Do you ever wish you'd listened to your mother and gone to law school?"

No one had ever taken over Lauren's office. Although four months had passed, her bright blue umbrella with the macrame strap still leaned in the corner next to the filing cabinet, her wool paisley Liberty scarf still dangled from the coatrack beside the door. Lauren's gradebook, course outlines, and book lists were stuffed higgledy-piggledy into her bookshelf just where she'd thrust them on the day of her death. Her tampons and maxipads still lay hidden in the back of the righthand desk drawer. Only the carpet had changed: maroon vinyl tile now covered the bloodstained floor where she'd lain.

Twice Ramona telephoned Mark Goldberg to remind him to remove Lauren's things. Both times the grief-stricken husband rambled on about his loss. "We had no children. Now I'm totally alone," he complained. Ramona had little patience with those who used business calls as an occasion for bereavement therapy.

"Who is Goldberg, anyway?" she asked Daphne. "I've never seen him."

"He's a sweater manufacturer. Lauren didn't bring him to department functions."

"No wonder."

"Simple," Daphne advised. "Just write a note and say everything will be destroyed if not picked up by January 1." She was eager to move into better quarters away from Lucille Streng. Ramona was not eager to be bossed by Daphne, and so the matter stood for six more weeks. Then one day a short bearded man stopped by the English office.

"Are you the departmental secretary?" He almost bowed. "I'm Mr. Goldberg. I need the key to my wife's office."

With a few deft strokes Ramona drew a map on a

memo pad to show Goldberg how to find East Science Faculty. She pressed the key into his hand while he murmured his thanks.

Ascending slowly in the elevator at ESF, Mark Goldberg passed a white handkerchief across his balding brow. He felt unsettled by the alien campus, the curt secretary, the unruly mobs of chattering students in odd tattered costumes. On the third floor Goldberg pressed uncertainly along the quiet darkened corridor like a miner exploring a new vein of coal. Here was the door of 309. Goldberg started at the loud click of the lock.

Once inside he threw himself into Lauren's chair and put his head in his hands. The tiny room was very cold and dank; air hissing in through the dusty grating seemed thick and used. She worked in *here*? Lauren had often complained about her chilly office, but he'd paid little attention. After a while Goldberg took a folded black trash bag from his jacket pocket and began filling it indiscriminately with Lauren's possessions. He worked quickly without pause for evaluation, his hands moving mechanically. He'd sort everything out at home.

When he reached the file cabinet stuffed with teaching materials, he stared, baffled for a few seconds, then began tossing the papers into the garbage can, which soon proved too small. After a moment's thought, he retrieved all the magazines and offprints and stacked them neatly in the corridor just outside the door, along with three piles of books, mostly uninviting grammar textbooks and fat anthologies of essays with student questions at the back. He kept a red leather *American Heritage Dictionary* with LAUREN GOLDBERG stamped in gold. Spotting a small canvas tote bag in the corner behind the student's chair, he drew out a tangle of knitting and several balls of yarn. This discovery caused him to weep, resting his head on the desk top for a long time.

Goldberg roused himself, wiped his tear-soaked beard with his handkerchief, combed his hair with the aid of Lauren's compact mirror. Then he worked on, bending and lifting, ripping up correspondence and student themes and tossing everything into the can. Finally only dust and paper clips remained in the drawers. Despite Goldberg's energetic activity, he still felt chilled; the room still felt like a tomb.

When cabinets and shelves were stripped, Goldberg stretched over the desk to the wall and carefully untacked Lauren's Japanese print of an *Iris ensata*. He rolled up the print and secured it with a rubber band. Then his eye fell on the green leather desk blotter embossed with tiny gold threads. Surely a blotter wasn't college property. As he lifted it, he saw a single sheet of creamy notepaper inscribed in Lauren's stubby, uneven hand. He read: "Dear George—I don't know why you've been behaving like this. I waited two hours for you to call me last night. I wish you'd be more straightforward with me. I can stand complaints but not coldness. Let's . . ."

Goldberg folded the sheet carefully twice and put it

in his inside jacket pocket. Then he turned and saw Lauren standing in the doorway, her red-blonde hair glowing from an invisible light source. "Why carry on like this?" she was saying in her familiar throaty voice, but in a light teasing tone. "*I'm* not making a fuss, so please, Mark, not you either." She smiled, revealing the seductive little gap between her top front teeth. "Have a little courage, man. After all, you're alive!"

Lauren faded for a moment, then brightened again. "As for George—it was only an experiment. Lighten up! You know it was you I always loved."

Goldberg stared, eyes bulging, but now saw only the chipped surface of the door and the scuffed doorknob. Trembling, he opened the door and slowly backed out, gripping the rolled-up print and the umbrella in one hand, the bulging trash bag in the other. The door click-locked behind him.

Outside, Goldberg found his escape route blocked by a tall trash barrel on wheels and a heavy woman bending over the stack of offprints—Elisabeth Hofrichter, just beginning her cleaning chores. She gave him a soft glance and moved aside. He did not know how surly she usually was.

"Pardon me, miss," he said, setting down the trash bag and extracting a five-dollar bill from his wallet. "This key to 309 belongs to the English department. Would you please return it for me? I'm not up to it right now."

The cleaning woman took the key and returned the money.

"I'm sorry for you, mister," she said. "I wish for you a better luck." She patted him once on the arm and began tossing Lauren's trash into the barrel. "Papers," she said as he staggered away down the hall. "Enough to bury the world. What good are they?"

When Steve went to the English office to pick up his mail, he was amazed to find Professor Reilly standing inside the little corral that held the secretaries, talking to Ramona. As far as Steve knew, George Reilly was supposed to be in Tucson, Arizona, recovering from a nervous breakdown. But George looked fit and rested. He'd grown his thick black hair into a small ponytail, which Steve, ten years younger, hadn't the nerve to do. His blue Polarfleece warm-up jacket, though casual, was new and spotless.

Steve didn't want to stare, so he hung around in front of the mailroom, pretending to read a departmental notice, his eyes spinning over these words while he strained to eavesdrop.

March 20, 1985
    FROM: Chair, English Department
    TO: ALL Fulltime Staff
    The next weekly meeting of the English

Department will take place on Thursday, March 28, at 1 P.M. The revised core program for British Writers Non-Arts Majors of the Modern Era (Prose) and Associate Degree Humanities Survey-Literature Component prerequisites, Tier II, will be voted upon.

"Does it have to be so dreary in here?" George was asking Ramona, but in a soft, charming voice, not at all in a confrontational way.

"Well, I'm here seven hours a day, don't you think I want it nice?" Ramona replied, a little acerbically, Steve thought, considering she was talking to a mental invalid. "The faculty just breeze in and out to pick up things. What do they want—the Plaza Hotel?"

"Perhaps a few geraniums on the windowsills." George's bright eyes were flicking up and down the dingy Temp 6 walls, which appeared to be cut from sheet metal. "A few colorful travel posters, Florence, Venice, and such. You can pick up terrific ones in the Village."

Ramona shook her head. "Since security etched the glass over, there's not enough light here for flowers. We have to keep the fluorescents on all the time. We have no budget for *posters*."

"And this shredded indoor-outdoor carpet, can't that be replaced?" George pawed it vigorously with his left Reebok. "It's hazardous, not just ugly."

"In the middle of a budget crisis?" Ramona cried. "When there's not enough money for ditto paper, and I have to rush over to Required Composition every time I need staples?"

George chuckled and passed back through the swinging gate to the public side of the English office, while Ramona leaned sideways against the ditto machine, her hands on what would pass for hips on another woman. She made a small sour face at his back.

"There are far too many grim things on this campus, don't you agree?"

Steve realized that George was addressing the question to him. Entranced by the conversation, he'd forgotten to pretend to be reading. George moved over and clapped him heartily on the back, as if he knew him well. They'd never spoken a word to each other before, as far as Steve could remember.

Was this the moment to reveal himself as George's replacement for the Joyce seminar? Would George then demand to see his recent lecture notes?

"You're silent. Does that mean you approve the squalor? We should all testify against ugliness." George's bold eyes roved over the seamy corners of the English office, probing the dark spaces beyond the filing cabinets, as if rats were about to spring out, then came to rest on Steve's flustered face. "If we don't squeak now and then, we'll have to spend the rest of our days with these horrors."

"It is an unusually ugly campus," Steve allowed, grinning idiotically. "All concrete and back alleys. Gray walls. Everything frayed or smudged."

George leaned over the rail to set his knapsack on Ramona's desk, then rummaged around inside. He pulled out a thick black leather volume, thumbed through its gilt-edged pages, then clapped his forefinger to a line. "Thou shalt not muzzle the ox that treadeth out the corn," he read aloud in a firm pleasant voice.

Oh, no, not recovered, Steve thought in panic.

"I'm glad you feel as I do. I appreciate your support." George turned back towards Ramona. "When the Chair comes in, please tell him I stopped off to see him and that I'll return. I'm eager to tell him about my plans for the future. With a little free time it's amazing how many new ideas arise."

He returned his gaze to Steve. "My master plan revitalizes the whole English department, you see, everything, course offerings, sequences, programming, the works. A few bugs to be worked out, and then I'll send it to President Cutter.

"Right now I'm heading for the gym," he added, tucking the Bible back into his knapsack. "You don't play tennis, do you? I need a partner."

"No," said Steve, feeling himself blushing for no reason he could think of. "I'm a swimmer. Unlike Stephen Dedalus, who was a hydrophobe . . . ," he babbled on with reddening face, wondering why he was dragging Joyce into the conversation when he'd decided to leave him out.

George wasn't interested in Stephen Dedalus. "Long legs often mean good tennis. I've got long legs myself."

He was right. Standing together, George and Steve matched exactly at shoulder and crotch. Both about the same weight (slim to skinny), they presented similar silhouettes except for the ponytail.

"When I was in your position in the department, new, I mean, I spent every afternoon in the gym and made lots of friends," George said in a mentor-like way.

Steve decided the best thing he could do was introduce himself. "I'm Steve Speck."

"I know that. I remember when you were hired. I wondered what it would be like to have the last name of a mass murderer."

At that moment, Allen Swain suddenly darted into the office. "Hi, Ramona," he called, waving a fat sheaf of purple-backed dittos in her direction. "More grist for your mill."

"Please drop them in the slot," she directed sternly. "Impossible to do right away. There's a mailing on new pension options due out yesterday. Gloria will put them in your mailbox tomorrow, Thursday at the latest."

Allen swivelled his head toward Steve and George. "Why, George Reilly," he said. "You're back. I didn't know you were back."

"Arrived from Arizona last night." George smiled thinly. Steve noted that he didn't clap Allen heartily on the back in greeting, but then Allen was almost a foot shorter. It would have been a hostile gesture.

"I'm well rested, full of pep. Better than ever. In fact, I'm running over to the gym now before I miss the action. I need exercise." He swung his knapsack on his shoulder and loped away without another word.

A few moments later, Steve and Allen trailed him down the corridor and saw his blue fleece back charging out the rear door. "Nice guy," Steve said with a sad shake of his head, "but still completely whacko."

"There's nothing wrong with him," Allen said firmly. "A bit excitable, always was a sort of hysterical type. It's to impress women. They love overstimulation. It's sexy."

Steve, puzzled, said nothing.

Inevitably the time for class observations rolled around, another big headache for the P & B Committee. The question was, should the P & B observe Cherry Binder along with the other nontenured members of the department? Normally, the committee wouldn't trouble to visit the terminated, who would simply be serving time till their departure. But Cherry was a special case. She'd already registered a grievance with the Brotherhood of College Teachers, a case she might or might not win. Cherry knew that she deserved tenure, the P & B knew she deserved tenure, but who knew how the president's office, the chancellor's office, or any outside arbitrator would rule?

"We need all the ammunition we can muster," said the Chair. "A negative observation can't hurt."

Daphne refused the assignment. She already had two other hatchet jobs to perform. Besides, Cherry's schedule didn't mesh conveniently with her own.

So the lot fell to Dickie, an eminently appropriate choice. This semester Cherry was trying a new course she'd designed and rammed through the Curriculum Committee—The English Novel as Feminist Document. Dickie was the departmental novel man as well as the departmental hatchet man. His expert opinion damning Cherry's worth as a teacher certainly would weigh heavily.

"But I gave her a smashing report on Virginia Woolf and Her Circle only last year!" Dickie objected.

"Don't get bogged down by details, Dickie," said the Chair. "That merely demonstrates your fair-mindedness. If you want to be an administrator, you have to see the figure in the carpet."

According to custom, Dickie left Cherry a little note in her mailbox: "I'll pop in to observe your novel class on Thursday." He gave her only two days' notice instead of the customary but not obligatory week.

Speedily, Cherry sent her reply. "See you Thursday. Too bad you won't have a chance to read *The Odd Women*, subject of classroom discussion, or hear my very important preparatory lecture." Cherry's note was scribbled on a blue-lined sheet torn from a notebook, little white dots of paper still clinging to the perforations.

"Tsk, tsk." Dickie always rejected student themes submitted on such low-grade paper. Had Cherry no respect for the author of "Anthony Trollope and the Irish Question"? Dickie was further inflamed to realize that Cherry was teaching a book that he enjoyed but had never found a way to fit into a syllabus of his own.

On Thursday Cherry began class a little early, as was her habit, so Dickie was obliged to slink into her crowded classroom and take his seat in the back with everyone's eyes fixed on him. It seemed to him that a number of students turned their heads to give him smoldering stares.

His perception was accurate. Cherry, never reticent, had revealed the state of affairs between herself and the department on the very first day of class. "You ought to know my position," she said with a haughty toss of her head as she handed out the book lists. "Fired without cause. I'm appealing, and I expect to be reinstated. But it's possible that this is the first and last time Feminist Novel will be given. My views are unpopular, but I hope you'll enjoy hearing them."

Sympathetic mutterings greeted her announcement. Then, to refresh the class's memory, Cherry had announced just before her *Odd Women* lecture, "Oh, by the way, next session I'm being observed by the department. I don't know why, since I'm being fired anyway."

Dickie felt uncomfortable and shifted nervously behind his plastic armrest. On his left Simon Kestenbaum, winner of the Luce Award for Junior Achievement at last year's prize ceremonies, was sending him a distinctly hostile stare, while Lucy Hawkins, his former star pupil in Fielding Through Smollett, turned her head toward the side blackboard, pretending he didn't exist. Dickie hadn't felt so unsettled since his first year of teaching when he was sure all his students despised him. He could barely pay attention to Cherry's utterances.

Cherry strode around the room as if she were wearing army boots, every eye following her. "The scene at the end of the novel where Rhoda and Everard meet for the last time—every time I read it I'm sitting up and panting. What makes it such hot stuff?"

Dickie shrank from the crudity of Cherry's expression, but he was interested to see how it jump-started the discussion. A forest of arms went up. Of the twenty-five or so people in ESF 101, at least twenty craved to answer.

"Because until the last moment you don't know if Rhoda will accept Everard . . . ," said Lucy.

"And worse," interrupted the girl beside her, "you don't know if she should accept him."

"Of course she shouldn't," another girl across the room broke in. "Because he's a bastard."

"But she loves him. And he's the only man who'll ever ask her to marry him, that's for sure."

"So, women," Cherry said tenderly, ignoring the ten or so men who sat in the room, "some of you think Rhoda should have bent her will to Everard, because he was the only man who'd ever been attracted to her. Was it to avoid a life without marriage, or to avoid a life without sex?"

"Sex, sex!" several people screamed out.

Cherry's voice grew lower, more seductive. "Sex, you know, is the only instinctive need you can live without."

"She's far better off without him," said Kestenbaum the Prize Winner authoritatively, also without raising his hand. Handraising was a dead form in this class. "He wanted to see if he had some power over her, that's the only reason he proposed. She did the right thing. She had her work. It wouldn't be a lonely life or an idle or unhappy life. Sex drive can be sublimated," he ended in a ringing tone.

Lucy jumped into the discussion. "I think that a celibate life might be dreary, but—"

Dickie Walter was entranced by these comments. He himself had lived a life without sex and was so drawn in by the liveliness of the discussion that he was tempted to remark from his seat in the back row that a sexless life could be perfectly happy, provided you were in touch with art, music, and literature, and had good health and enough money for travel, concert tickets, and restaurant meals.

"But *The Odd Women* was written by a man. What did Gissing know about women's sexual needs?" Cherry flung out the question and twenty-five students fought to answer it.

After class Dickie stopped by Cherry's desk to proffer a few gentlemanly words of thanks, his immutable custom, for it had always been the drill at Harvard College. He was hard put to know what else to say.

"Excellent choice of novel," he pronounced, resting his green book bag for the moment on the Formica desk top. "Time constraints usually force me to drop Gissing from my list. When feasible, but rarely, I include *New Grub Street*. I assume your previous lecture dissected the life of Gissing and laid bare all connections with nineteenth-century narrative?"

"Sure, I hit all the right buttons," Cherry replied with a rude stare.

Dickie made a note to use "crude" or "unpolished" in his report.

"You must excuse me," Cherry said, piling her many volumes into her briefcase and turning away. "I have an infant and a lover waiting for me at home."

Cherry, however, was not as happy and confident as

her words to Dickie would suggest. In her journal she
wrote

> Till now I've never been subject to those neu-
> rotic bouts of self-doubt afflicting my fellow intellec-
> tuals and fellow women. (Can I *say* "fellow
> women"?) But my last chapter has an artificial ring,
> no bite at all.
>
> I know it's not a lack of energy from caring for
> Morley. Morley has energized me! When Norman
> was with me, I wrote every single day. While he
> vacuumed or did the accounts, the prose churned
> out of me. I wrote *Green Wives* in only six months!
>
> Could he have been an invigorating influ-
> ence? Unlikely. Probably it's the strain of dealing
> with Sally, or all the stupidities going on at Muni.
> Still, the work does not go forward. I must get on
> top of it soon. I need the book for a better job! Go
> forward, go forward, go forward!

in her impetuous handwriting, the letters slanting forward at an alarming angle.

Dealing with Sally was the top priority, Cherry
decided. It was amazing how fast a simple desire-driven
relationship had metamorphosed into a complex psycho-
logical mess. Sally had grown amazingly querulous. It was
one thing to lie cuddled in bed with Sally and another to

hear her complaints and entreaties every minute of the livelong day. Sally was always trying to influence or manipulate, to lure Cherry into staying overnight with her in Brooklyn, to eat Sally's favorite vegetarian dish, listen to her favorite singer, drink from her favorite teacup. And whenever Sally stayed with Cherry on West Ninety-sixth Street, she would be sniping and blathering about the same topic: cleaning up the apartment.

No one looking at Cherry herself, with her white strong teeth, fat glossy leather briefcase, and crisp shirt from the Chinese laundry, would ever guess that pools of green scum lay on the bottom of her refrigerator, that brown crusts ringed the electric burners of her stove, that ancient pink cotton panties mildewed in her laundry bag. The square brown roach traps in the corners of her kitchen were veiled with filth, the grillwork at the bottom of the fridge furred with thick gray dust, the inside of the shower curtain splotched with black.

Since Cherry hated to clean and didn't believe in exploiting sisters to do the work she loathed, Norman had always done the cleaning. When Norman left for Dallas, the apartment became a cesspit. This deterioration didn't bother Cherry. She hardly noticed. More important matters occupied her mind, that is, until Sally began complaining.

Only last week they'd quarreled about the bottom of the garbage can.

"You've got a whole new species growing in here!" Sally remarked, trying the humorous vein first.

"Mmm." Cherry was drinking coffee at the kitchen counter and thinking hard about her meeting with officials of the Brotherhood of College Teachers that afternoon.

"Aren't you going to do something about it? Yuck, it's just utterly yuck. I can't stand looking at it."

"Mmm." Cherry blinked her eyes rapidly, signifying, I'm not paying attention.

Oblivious, Sally hoisted up the can and brought it over to where Cherry was sitting, rattling the lid. "Take a look! It's going to reach out and grab us."

"*Will* you please be quiet," Cherry said in a tone Sally hadn't heard before. "I'm trying to think, in case you haven't noticed."

"You're living in filth! Unhealthiness everywhere! Dust, grime, germs, spores, mold . . . don't you care about Morley's health?"

"Why are you poking your nose in my garbage can? Have you no notion of privacy? You'll be reading my letters next."

"Jesus, Cherry, you are one unreasonable bitch!"

"When I have something serious on my mind, do I need you to pester me about some stupidity?"

"Stupidity?" Sally burst into tears. "You treat me like shit, that's the stupidity."

When Sally slammed out, Cherry felt relief, followed by a certain annoyance. Why all this fuss and bother? Within an hour Sally was on the phone with apologies and a desire to meet "to discuss our intimacy with cooler heads."

After sidestepping Sally for a while with pleas of heavy workloads and imminent deadlines, Cherry finally agreed to meet for lunch between classes at Muni. It was far easier to communicate within the restraints of the academic community. No hugging and kissing, for one thing. No tears.

As she approached Cherry's table in the lunchroom, Sally looked pale and subdued, far from the dynamic self-possessed young woman Cherry had first met a few months ago at the honors reception. Only twenty-six, in her fretful state she looked ten years older, her olive skin tinged with yellow, mauve shadows under her eyes.

"When I don't see you for a few days I feel empty," Sally began with a dim smile.

Cherry was silent. It was impossible to respond to such an exaggerated statement.

"Why can't you and Morley live with me? It's the only solution." Sally had a large flat on a pleasant tree-lined street in Brooklyn. "We belong together!"

"Sally, why torment yourself? What's wrong with our present relationship? We see each other lots. We're close. What's the problem?"

"Please don't give me such horrible looks!"

Sally and Cherry were sitting only a few tables away from three members of the P & B enjoying a convivial lunch. Also, Gordon Fosco of romance languages was leaning forward in his chair, almost within earshot. For this reason, the lovers' dialogue was muted, their glances powerful.

"It's not such a bizarre wish, to be with the one you love, to be intimate," Sally whispered.

"What is intimacy? Living up someone else's nose."

"God, Cherry, you're so crass."

"I'm just trying to make my point in pungent language. I'm not as refined as you think I am. Let me be blunt. I need emotional space. I don't want to get taken over by you, which is what moving to Park Slope would be. If you want to be with me" (here Cherry was aware she was going much further than she'd ever intended, moved against her will by Sally's sad obsession) "you know you're welcome to stay with *me* any time."

"In that tiny apartment?"

"In that tiny apartment. I feel comfortable there and that's where I want to be."

"Okay. I'll sublet. I don't think it's the best plan, but I'm willing to try it. Once I sublet, though, you know I can't go back there."

This was the sort of blackmail Cherry feared. "I have nibbles from Oberlin. They may need me for a two-year contract. I may move to Ohio if I can't find anything tenure-track. Or somewhere else."

"You'd let me sublet and then move away? You'd do that to me?"

Cherry regarded Sally with a sober appraising eye. "That's why I'm telling you now. I'm not looking for a life partner, Sally. I already have one, remember?"

Sally stared down at her carrot salad. She found another tack, one she'd tried several times before. "You know I can't stay in your apartment until you hire a cleaning person."

"I have told you one hundred times," Cherry articulated with stiffened lips, "why I can't hire another woman, probably black, to clean up my dirt."

"You'd rather have me do it."

"Yes, if you're so fastidious." For the first time in a long while, Cherry longed for Norman, who simply did the housework instead of arguing.

"What a holier-than-thou you are, Miss Piggy."

They exchanged murderous looks, while Cherry tried to think of an annihilating comeback.

"What kind of cabal is Cherry cooking up with the French department?" said Quinton from his vantage point nearby. "Maybe she's looking for some kind of comp lit connection."

"Whatever it is, it's to her own advantage," Daphne said virtuously.

"Such ferocity! Look how her eyes flash! That girl should be in the president's office." Dickie sent her an admiring glance.

"In a steel cage," said Quinton.

"I'll drink to that." Daphne raised her water in its dull tumbler.

And they all smiled and toasted Cherry Binder.

I'm starting to feel like an old man. I never used to worry about things so much, Steve thought, as he checked his notes, his attendance sheets and his grade-book for the third time. Mary Burnson was coming to observe his Joyce elective in a few minutes, and though she seemed like a good-hearted person, he didn't have high hopes of a brilliant class. Why couldn't she come to his lively freshman class?

Why did a guy like Brett Feinman want to take a Joyce class when he already knew all about Joyce? Why didn't he take *The Faerie Queene* or *Sir Gawain and the Green Knight*?

Steve had spotted trouble on the very first day when this sandy-haired fellow with sparse blond beard and rounded shoulders had begun asking intelligent questions about the reading list, an unheard-of undergraduate scenario. Ordinarily students were empty vessels waiting to be filled, but from day one, Feinman overflowed with facts about James Joyce, most of them news to Steve.

So far Steve by huge expenditure of time and effort had prepared some decent scholarly lectures. *Ulysses*, the real difficulty, had been pushed off to the end of the term while Steve lingered lovingly on *Dubliners* and *Portrait of the Artist*. But Feinman was always leaping ahead, asking pointed questions about *Ulysses*. At first it was hard to tell if he was seeking knowledge or just trying to make Steve look like a fool. Lately Feinman's questions had shown more than a trace of impatience and a dollop of insolence as well. Steve was getting rattled.

Here was Mary Burnson in the doorway, her long sheep's face looking intense and harried. She waved at Steve. With many flutterings of her silky poncho-like garment she settled herself into the back row under the coat hooks with a yellow legal pad and three sharpened pencils. His incoming students would spot her immediately and either freeze up or make heroic efforts to save Steve's ass. Steve was touched by how often even the most marginal student made that generous gesture.

Several young women entered the classroom, bestowing on Steve bright smiles of welcome. Then in sauntered Brett Feinman, a wispy youth of about twenty-one, thinner than Steve, if this was possible. Seated in the front row he ostentatiously pulled out the *New York Times*. By the way he slapped the pages together, whack/whack, whack/whack, Steve knew trouble lay ahead.

Steve's opening lecture on *Portrait of the Artist* was a

model of elegant organization. He described the haunting scene at the end of chapter four when Stephen visits a prostitute and feels "an unknown and timid pressure, darker than the swoon of sin, softer than sound or odor."

"Gorgeous metaphor, but sex is ultimately too 'dark and vague,' not articulate enough for the poet in Joyce," Steve said, stealing a glance at Mary in the back row. How was this modest person taking his sexual references? Her face only showed eager interest.

Feinman's hand shot up. "Joyce picked up VD from these prostitutes. That was the cause of his later eye problems."

"Oh," said Steve innocently. "I never heard that. Ellmann says it was glaucoma."

Feinman gave a terse laugh. "It was untreated syphilis," he insisted.

"A fascinating thought," Steve went on, "but I'm still skeptical. Ellmann would have mentioned it in his biography. He's so thorough. He researched that book *twice*. It's crammed with details about doctors' visits, operations, diagnoses."

Feinman grinned. "I'm surprised you're not aware of this, Professor Speck. It's the latest critical scoop. Ellmann doesn't know *everything*—and neither do you."

Steve flushed scarlet. He literally didn't know what to say. A long moment passed.

To his surprise, Mary spoke up from the back row. "Syphilis among romantic poets was ever so common. I've often thought of writing an article on the subject, but my medical knowledge is skimpy."

"It does seem that every other artist in the nineteenth century was syphilitic," Steve allowed.

Other students began naming names.

"Manet."

"Schubert!"

"Heine."

"Nietzsche?"

"De Maupassant!"

"Beethoven!"

During this conversation Feinman had somehow lost the center of the stage and lost interest in annoying Steve. He slumped in his seat and didn't say another word that hour.

After class Mary came up and chatted with a sweet smile on her face. "You handled that intrusive student *beautifully*," she said, though Steve hadn't handled anything. "And you know, I think that fellow was making it up as he went along, just to damage you. I wonder why he would do that, when you're so obviously an excellent teacher."

Steve felt bathed in happiness. I love you, Mary Burnson. If you were only young and beautiful, I'd ask you to marry me right now. If only you didn't look like a giant garden insect in your washed silk poncho, I'd spend my life with you!

Anyone could tell this would be no humdrum P & B meeting simply by glancing at the Chair's sunny face as he bounced into the library meeting room. His normally crimson complexion had faded to a uniform rose, and even the pink scalp visible in the parting of his silvery hair held the vigorous glow of health.

When seated, he threw beaming glances across the table at Lucille, whom he usually ignored. "Heavenly day," he said, though no ray of light ever penetrated these basement depths.

"It's colder than last March. This morning I was looking at the thermometer on my porch . . ." Lucille began one of her interminable historical weather reviews, but the Chair didn't fidget with his pencils and folders. He heard her out with a smile. When Dickie straggled in a few minutes later, the Chair beamed the same indulgent smile.

"Now that we're all assembled, let me begin with some wonderful albeit unexpected news—one might say, a bombshell. To take extraordinary measures to combat the budget deficit, the board of trustees has been empowered, and this only last night—I heard it from my informant in the chancellor's office, so you won't have heard a word about it—to offer all full professors with more than twenty years of service an extra four years of retirement credit if they choose early retirement within the next month!"

The other P & B members looked blank. It was hard to see what was so wonderful about this news. Daphne shrugged. She had fifteen and a half years of service. So what.

Dickie sighed. He'd served twenty-two years, but having gone overboard buying bibelots in London last summer, he couldn't dream of retiring early. The Georgian fish slice and the set of twelve Royal Dairy demitasse had fully mortgaged this semester. Not to mention the 1868 church pew cum brass umbrella holder.

On the other side of the table, Lucille returned an antagonistic glare. She was young yet. Teaching English was her life's blood. While ignorant students stalked a campus rife with grammatical error, the board would never get her to retire, never!

"My personal news is that I shall take special retirement leave at the end of the semester and receive my pension officially next January 1."

"For heaven's sake!" Lucille gawked. "You're going to give up your Chair?"

"My dear, I haven't been elected for my second term yet, and this saves me the trouble of running. While you're toiling and moiling here, I'll be growing juicy red tomatoes in my garden in East Hampton. You, Quinton," he said waggishly, "are the Chair Apparent. Your warm cries of congratulations are the ones I most expected to hear."

Quinton had been sitting glumly in the seat farthest from the Chair, staring at his fleshy fingertips, his face in shadow, his bulky body motionless. When he looked up, he seemed anything but pleased.

"Bad timing, Ed. I also have some news to tell. As of the fall semester, I'll be heading the graduate program at NYU."

Baleful silence greeted his words. No one congratulated Quinton for his step upward, actually two steps upward. The Chair's incandescent smile vanished. His face reddened to its normal apoplectic hue. "I only wish you'd *told* me. Was it necessary to be so secretive? No transition? No grooming? No coordination? It's not what I'd call team playing. After all, *my* news was unexpected."

Quinton fretfully pulled his moustache. "I planned to tell you as soon as a firm offer was made, but NYU kept me dangling for months. I had no great hopes, to tell the truth. If you'd given me one hint of your retirement, I might not have applied. Why didn't you warn me you might leave?"

"Well, well." The Chair put a good face on it. Who here could fault Quinton for being ambitious? He nodded. "We're both simply following our stars."

"What about the continuity of the department?" Daphne said in her usual accusatorial tone. She whipped her head back and forth to include both the Chair and Quinton in her righteous glare. "With both of you leaving at the same moment, chaos ensues. Who knows what will happen now?" She wrung her blue-veined hands.

"And what about the P & B?" added Dickie. "Without you, our program, our blueprint for the department, everything we've been struggling for, all goes down the drain."

Lucille looked puzzled. What blueprint did he mean?

"Certainly we'll arrange for continuity, good continuity, total continuity," the Chair responded with spirit.

"Exactly how?"

"Exactly this way. One of you will succeed me as Chair. Throwing open the election will only ensure chaos, as you say!"

The three possible Chairs at the table looked at one another with interest. "I never wanted to be Chair, but I'll step in and fulfill my responsibility," Daphne said briskly.

Nobody replied. Daphne fulfilling her responsibility was a wholly depressing prospect.

"What about Proctor?" Quinton suggested. "True, he's in Australia, but it's possible to conduct an effective long-distance campaign. He's popular. He's capable. He's already one of us."

Lucille, who only served on the P & B as temporary replacement for Harve Proctor, looked cheerful. Perhaps this maneuver would bring her a permanent spot.

The Chair shifted round in his chair, his forehead wrinkling for the first time this morning. "That's impossible. Normally I wouldn't divulge this." He looked around the table at the extra-alert faces of his colleagues. "If you can keep this to yourselves . . ."

All nodded vigorously.

"Harve is in trouble. I was contacted by his chairman there to find out if he'd ever been in trouble *here*."

"What sort of trouble?" Quinton asked, scenting a wonderful scandal.

"Sexual harassment, brought by no fewer than three students. And he's only been there six months." The Chair was pained to note that this news caused a far greater uproar than word of his retirement. Everyone began talking at once.

"Badly handled . . . Australian hair-trigger temper . . . Damaging, very damaging . . . Up to his old tricks . . ."

"So you see, I don't want a word of this matter to go beyond these walls." The Chair stared at the dusty plaster. "I rely on your discretion."

"Under these circumstances," Quinton said with a return of his old vigor, "I nominate Daphne, whose administrative capacities are well known. We've never had a woman Chair."

"Yes, we did," the Chair recalled. "Hortense Leary, now with the NEH. She was elected in the late sixties, but she never served. A call from Washington and she rose like a rocket. But I agree. Daphne is our only choice. You'll give them hell, Daphne."

Daphne smiled and touched her greying helmet as if putting on a diadem. "I accept. Dickie, you'll be associate chair. And of course you'll be Chair after me," she added graciously.

"Shouldn't I go first? Two terms from now I'll be much too old."

"Nonsense. You're eternally young, Dickie."

"An advisory role best suits your talents," Quinton added in silky tones, meaning, I can't see *you* tangling with the administration.

"I'd be glad for the number-two spot," Lucille said.

"Dickie, I promise to rely on you absolutely." Daphne stared into her friend's thick spectacles. "Except of course when you're on your sabbatical, which I'm sure we can arrange as early as next semester."

Dickie took off his glasses, thought for a second, then subsided with a nod.

Daphne now turned to glare at Lucille. "Two women in charge of the department at one time—out of the question!" she snapped.

"A speedy transfer is what I aim for." The Chair, back in his sunny mode, beamed. "The P & B will continue to run as harmoniously as it does now."

"Aren't you forgetting the election?" Daphne began rustling through her papers, looking for her copy of the academic calendar. "Let's set the date as soon as possible. Let the department see it as a mere formality. Don't give other candidates time for fiddle-faddle."

"Right now we don't even know who the opposition is," Quinton pointed out.

"Allen Swain," Lucille put in triumphantly. "I overheard Mary Burnson blabbing about him in the ladies'. He wants desperately to be Chair. He's been approaching people for months."

All chuckled.

"An unappetizing prospect," said Daphne. "And what has he ever done for the department that he has the right to solicit votes?"

The Chair glanced at his own calendar. "Three weeks from today—absolute minimum."

"But that's when the department gets together for the grade-in," Daphne objected. "The proficiency exams can't wait around to be graded. And what about the department party? Isn't that always the week before the election?"

"Actually, I thought of cancelling the party this year. Our most defensible budget cut."

"Shortsighted, Ed," Daphne complained. "The party is too useful for interpersonal dealings. And it doesn't really cost much. Some wine, some cheese, a few napkins."

"I have a thought," said Quinton, who'd snapped

out of his glum mood. "Here we have three obligatory occasions for the department to get together. In the name of budget, let's combine the grade-in, the departmental party, and the election all on the same day. It'll save money and also wear and tear on us. We won't have to come dragging in time and again, and we'll accomplish everything in one blow. It will also solve the problem of grade-in absenteeism."

"Brilliant! This way we can also eliminate departmental spouses. They're the ones I regret spending money on." The Chair wrinkled his forehead again. "It's great pity you're going to NYU, Quint. I hate to think of losing that innovative mind."

"Sounds dangerous to me," Dickie piped up, still smarting from Quinton's comment about "an advisory role." "Combining functions indiscriminately like that, we run the risk of wrecking everything. Don't forget we serve alcohol at that party."

"That's simple. Don't open the bar till we've finished grading the proficiency exams."

"But then they'll be drinking before the department meeting."

"I don't know what we can do about that. If we have the election immediately after the grade-in, everyone will be hungry and irritable."

"It's only wine and cheese—no cocktails," Daphne reminded.

"I guess that will be all right. Nothing too wicked can happen."

Word of the Chair's retirement spread with sensational speed. Allen Swain heard about it just before he stepped into Spotlight on French Cinema. He gave his most lively lecture in years, dancing about on the podium with his pointer raised. Then he retired to the men's room to smile at himself in the mirror. Never had he imagined the Chair and Quinton both blown away at the same moment.

Steve in his outsider's role felt only lackluster interest. He'd spoken to the Chair once only, the day he was hired, but Quinton had selected him from the ranks to fill George's spot, so he felt a drop of sorrow at losing a superior officer who knew his name.

Brian, sitting at a table for one in the faculty lunchroom, felt weak with relief. If Daphne became Chair, his job was saved. He decided to postpone sending out more job applications.

Ramona wept.

Cherry and Morley were out of town attending a weight-challenged-women's conference, but Allen left an ecstatic message on Cherry's answering machine, which was sure to cheer her up on her return.

Later that afternoon the Chair and Quinton walked over to the faculty lounge for some tea and Social Tea Biscuits, a break they rarely enjoyed.

"We're well out of it." The Chair chuckled. "Leave it all to Daphne." He chuckled even louder. "Ramona will be wild."

"It's nice not to be next in line anymore," Quinton allowed. "I feel free for the first time."

"But you'll miss all this, won't you?" The Chair gestured toward the barren quad, the college flagpole stuck in its concrete base, a traffic barrier of orange plastic, the back door of Madison tied shut with a rope.

"Like you miss a sore tooth, like you miss an abscess. If I'd known then what I know now about the workings of Muni, I never would've applied."

"Don't get all sloppy and sentimental about it."

Both men guffawed.

7

Steve was beginning to wise up. If he was ever going to have a permanent job, he'd better starting paying attention to his career. Getting tired of being marginal, he mused. You need a network of helpful friends. You've always been a loner, and for what? So you can read more books than other people?

In keeping with his resolve to take stricter care of himself and his career, Steve called Cherry a few days before the grade-in and requested a lift to Muni at 8:30 A.M. He'd never asked her for a ride in the daytime before.

"If I go by subway, I'll have to get up at the crack of dawn."

"If you must know," Cherry replied, in something of a huff, "I'm not planning to show up till the department meeting. I'm boycotting the grade-in. Why should I work for free? I'm surprised you're even *thinking* of it. Other schools pay teachers to grade entrance exams. They pay well. And *you* don't even have a permanent appointment! Why would you appear?"

"To advance my career," Steve said boldly, throwing himself into his new role. "To show myself so I won't be forgotten. To charm the powers that be."

Cherry gave a scornful sniff. "A rotten way to advance your career. You think those little shits will remember you two minutes after exploiting you? You're an unpaid slave. Recognize that fact, man. Know who you're dealing with."

"Whom," said Steve, sealing his fate as far as Cherry was concerned.

In bed that night Steve groaned to Aimee. "Oh, God, how can I make it out there by 9 A.M.? Why can't they start at a decent hour? Also it's rush hour. I didn't become an English teacher to ride around the subways in rush hour."

Aimee had taken space in an artists' studio on Broome Street. Steve found that they got along better when they weren't together every minute of the day. Aimee offered to borrow her father's Chrysler, which sat in a garage most of the winter, and drive Steve out to Muni so he wouldn't have to get up at the crack of dawn. The crack of dawn was frightening to Aimee.

"Sweetie, I adore you. That's such an unselfish idea. You know, under normal circumstances you'd be coming to the department party with me, but they're not having spouses this year."

Aimee, pleased to be mentioned in the spouse category, snuggled closer to Steve. "Maybe I should wait for you and drive you back?"

"No, of course not. It'll take hours, and the Muni campus is a desert."

"I could wait in your office and do my needlepoint." She wiped her bare toes against the backs of his thighs and calves and he giggled.

"Well, okay, if you insist . . . That Cherry is really something," he mumbled dreamily. "Tough as nails."

"Are you attracted to her?"

"Not in the way you think." He grabbed Aimee and hoisted her against his chest. "She'd be an armful. I can't see myself doing this with her," he said, wrestling Aimee around to his other side under the covers, not without some difficulty. "Well, maybe if I were in the army or a prison camp or something. She'd be good as an army buddy to carry my machine gun."

"I don't believe you. And you don't have any machine gun."

"Oh, no?" He pushed against her, laughing. "Anyway, she's married, so you can relax. And she thinks I'm weak and spineless, and mewling and puking."

"You're not?"

Steve began to maul her in a semirealistic way, and they soon stopped using human speech.

Academic life is so predictable, said Mary Burnson to herself as she left the elevator at the top floor of the student union at 8:59 A.M., carrying the cardboardy tea and the cranberry muffin she knew she would need to get her through the morning.

I've done this grade-in so many times and it's always exactly the same. The essays are stupid and pathetic and the others are nasty about it and make jokes at the poor students' expense. The overhead lighting is harsh, and my eyes feel as though they're about to drop out.

She crossed the dark corridor heading toward the brighter meeting room. The space for large gatherings was infinitely flexible with many folding panels that could be pushed aside for an overflow crowd or pulled forward to camouflage a tiny turnout for a visiting poet. Stacks of metal folding chairs lined the walls.

When Mary entered the drafty, blue-carpeted grading area, not one other professor was in sight, not even Lucille Streng, the director of the event. A few graduate assistants sat huddled at a distant table. The view from the tall drafty window showed the ugly towers of Humanities, the Mordecai Raskin Memorial Library built in the shape of half a doughnut, and the gray lawns and gray concrete of the campus. The American flag set in a concrete base in the middle of the quad whipped Manhattanward in a stiff wind.

A familiar bleak feeling settled over Mary as she

doffed her damp trenchcoat and tried to hang it on the still-bare rack. The coat kept slipping off the flimsy wire hanger onto the floor. On the last downward slide it fell on the tea container Mary had set on the floor and knocked it over. Oh, darn. Darn. There was an ugly spreading stain on her trenchcoat. She always tried to do the right thing, and what was her reward?

Every year since the grade-in began (1968: the gathering was dubbed "grade-in" after the college teach-in on Vietnam), all participants had grumbled about its early starting time. Way too early, everyone said. Sleep still in our eyes, how can we make important judgments? Maurice el-Okdah had proposed changing the hour a half dozen times at department meetings, and always the distinguished scholar was overruled on the grounds that the enormous number of essays required a prompt beginning. Lucille drafted a notice to that effect. "Due to the large number of proficiency essays . . ." "Due to" is not an English construction," grumbled el-Okdah.

Despite exhortations and reminders stuffed into mailboxes hardly anyone ever did turn up promptly. (Once George Reilly appeared, but he'd written down the wrong time.) Mary was usually the first.

With a shudder Mary spotted Lucille sweeping toward the grading area trailed by Harry Rhett carrying a huge stack of exam books. "Where's Heidi?" Lucille barked, and Heidi Weismuller scurried out from behind a panel in a posture of obedience.

Next year I'll cut. I won't appear at all. I'll manumit myself, Mary vowed. She sat down at the nearest table and peeled the plastic wrap from her muffin and took an oversize bite. The pale light shining through the tall windows fell on her pale face with its prominent nose and sad expression.

The P & B will never promote me, anyway, no matter what I do to please them. You'd think "Fire and Flame in Shelley" would have done the trick, but no, the Chair thought it was derivative. I swear next year I'll definitely cut.

But even while Mary chewed on her dry muffin crumbs, she knew she was afraid not to show up, and that no matter how earnestly she vowed, she would always be there on time.

When he saw Daphne beckoning him from a corner as he walked through the shadowy outer meeting room, Brian felt like running back to the elevators. What now?

"Will you nominate me?" Daphne said, as if asking him to dance. For the campaign and party Daphne had changed her combative gladiator's hairdo to a poodle cut of close-cropped curls. Because the severe face below the curls held deep pursed wrinkles around the mouth, Daphne appeared to be passing negative judgment on her own hairstyle.

"Dickie says it would look better if the nomination doesn't come from a P & B member," she continued. "Just say my name in a dignified way. Everyone already knows I'm the candidate, so there's no need for a little speech. Your proposing me will also go down well with the younger people."

In a dignified way. Up till now, Brian had never really classified his feelings about Daphne. When she'd shown a marked preference for him early in his career at Muni, he'd followed her without question, taking her orders no matter how obscure. Later, when it looked as though she couldn't save him from being fired, he'd followed her anyway. Now that she was on her way to being Chair, he followed her and hated her, too. He knew she was not really as omniscient as she pretended. He'd done more for her than she had ever done for him.

"Just as you say." Brian produced his forthright, manly grin, but gave Daphne a little less wattage than usual. He was tired of being manipulated. He thought with longing of his senior year at Lehigh, going out to Richie's pinball arcade after the library with his roommate, Fred. One night he'd won fifty free games.

"I see that Murray el-Okdah is sitting at your table. We can't figure out which way he's going. Maybe you can sound him out."

"Okay, Daphne."

"I see Cherry is taking the day off. Attendance at the grade-in is mandatory! Next time the election will be at the last department meeting. I will insist upon it. The program today is preposterous."

Brian watched Daphne's lip pucker as she pronounced each "p" word. As the lips moved up and down, he thought of sewing them together.

"The P & B was potty, if you ask me." Daphne frowned. "The party should be purely for pleasure."

If Daphne won the election, Brian was likely to keep his job. Nonetheless, keeping his job at this point seemed like a terrible punishment. He stood alone for a minute after Daphne wheeled off to pester someone else. How long until he was a P & B member and could stop taking orders? Maybe never. Someday perhaps he would be Chair, but he'd never survive till that distant time.

Brian slid into place at table number five beside Mary Burnson. She looked almost as glum as he felt, her head slumped forward on her hand, her shoulders hunched. As soon as she saw him, though, she straightened and brightened, flashing a supportive smile.

"'Lo, Brian. How does it go with you?"

"I'm still asleep. I'm not ready for this." I'm not ready for *you*, he meant. He hoped she'd just sit there like a fellow zombie and forget about conversation, but Mary turned her full face toward him for a chat.

"I don't know," Mary said. "This routine gets harder and harder every year. There must be a better way to place freshmen. Why not simply assign them to English 1 classes and let their teachers weed out the unprepared ones for remedial classes?"

You birdbrain, Brian thought, but he replied politely,

"How'd you know how many remedial classes to offer if you don't read essays the term before? A scheduling nightmare! Hiring half-alive part-timers at the last minute if you guessed wrong. All kinds of transferring students trekking hither and thither. Unequal rosters! Madness!"

"Oh, that's right—*you* schedule classes," Mary said with a happy smile. "I don't know how you do such a wonderful job with such a complicated task."

Brian gave her his 250-watt smile. "Also," he continued in warmer tones, "the senior staff doesn't teach English 1, so the part-timers and junior people would be making all the decisions about standards for the whole department. This could result in lowering standards."

"They can't get much lower, can they?" Mary said with a grim honesty he didn't expect. "And what's wrong with the junior people making some decisions?"

Although Mary was tenured and years older than he was, Brian recalled, she was still at his own junior rank, assistant professor. If *she's* that critical of the department, poor featherweight, I wonder how the more rebellious ones are feeling? *She* won't be voting for Daphne, he thought with a stab of envy.

He shifted his aviator frames away from his restless eyes and blew on them the hot breath of frustration. "So I take it you're for Allen?"

"In the election? Well, I'm still at sea. I'm certainly for change, but do you really think Allen Swain can do better?"

Brian shrugged and scrubbed at his glasses with a clean handkerchief.

With a loud rattle Heidi Weismuller and Betsy Fuller whipped into the room wheeling a steel trolley topped by a giant coffee urn. A small man from the cafeteria followed, carrying a cardboard box with milk, sugar, and cups. Behind him bustled Lucille with napkins and stirrers and what looked like a box of graham crackers.

"Incredible," Mary said. "They're going to serve us coffee!"

"That's because there's an election coming up. Isn't it nice to be courted?"

It wasn't much of a critical remark, but Brian had never said anything about the department before, had never been anything but an official mouthpiece. It felt good to relax his rigid control and to let his mouth quack on.

Together Mary and Brian rushed to the hastily arranged table near the window. "I try to stay away from coffee," Mary said, "but sometimes one needs a jolt."

"I need more than a jolt, I need a cataclysm. Reading student drivel all morning, then an election, then teaching at night." And then an empty apartment with empty twin cribs, an empty refrigerator, empty bed. Crafty Cynthia, unhappy about her thwarted attempts at revenge at Muni, had written a note to Tiffany, a simple devastating blow. "Thanks for the loan of your husband." Tiffany packed up and left that very day, leaving the note pinned to the refrigerator door with a magnet in the shape of a pig.

Bright sunlight suddenly fell through the top floor windows of the student union. One ray fell on Mary's golden hair swept back from her face with a black velvet ribbon, hair as fine as the golden wires in a Renaissance portrait. Mary did resemble a Renaissance woman, with her big nose, high forehead, thin arched brows, curving cheeks, and tiny hint of another chin. She had a sort of squarish neckline to her dress from which emerged a faint perfume.

"You look like Elizabeth of York," Brian said suddenly, staring down at Mary over his Styrofoam cup. "You know, the one in the National Portrait Gallery in London. She's holding a rose?"

Mary shook her head. Brian was certainly acting strangely today, totally unlike his usual bland, remote self. She peered at him curiously. "Was she one who got her head cut off?"

"No, indeed."

Brian realized that, whether she knew it or not, Mary would like nothing better than for him to make love to her. Let's have a quickie in the supply closet, he imagined saying and chuckled to himself, but soon discovered that just the thought of touching Mary was bringing the blood to his crotch. God, he was horny. Abandoned by both wife and girlfriend, he was starved for sex. Oh, oh.

In obedience to nature, but in sight of the whole English department, his penis stirred and engorged. He quickly sought some random fantasy to reduce his readiness.

Daphne was there, naked, in the supply closet. Her flesh rippled down her front in folds, sagging breasts, sagging belly, even sagging vulva, though that may have been a trick of the light. Daphne's rippling, corrugated thighs reminded him of rotting locust wood posts he'd once dug up from the wet sand beneath a deck. He imagined the wet sucking sound of the locust posts being pulled out of the sand, but this, unfortunately, started him off again.

Daphne, yes, her skinny wormy body, the perfect turnoff. Most repellent of all, the speckled spotted flesh. Little mottled flecks of brown, red, gray, every sort of spot grown on flesh grew on Daphne's chest and long skinny arms. She approached him, back arched, arms outstretched, tilting her pubis as a lure and challenge. He gagged, turned aside. Next she reached behind her for a knotted rope, the cat-o'-nine-tails, and swung it through the air, catching him on the temple. He reached up, felt spurting blood. She grabbed his hand and pushed it between her legs. He felt the warm gooey crevice. His prick rose up and he stuck it in. "Bravo, Brian, I knew I could make you my sex slave," Daphne slavered in her crisp British accent, rubbing her riding whip across his carotid artery.

Brian's fixated gaze drew Mary's attention.

"Anything wrong?" Mary's timid question brought a feverish flush to Brian's already ruddy face.

"No, not at all," Brian answered, but his averted glance gave Mary a mild whiff of sexuality.

She peeped at his by now enormous crotch and blushed, feeling herself energized and half-amazed. He's married, but perhaps his marriage is on the rocks. He's sort of beefy. (She preferred pale intellectual types like George with long sensitive fingers and swanlike necks.) Quite the satyr, she thought, as the loose-fitting gray trousers which were designed to cover up just such contingencies bulged bigger each second. Where will this end?

Since Daphne's elderly body was clearly not a viable stopper, Brian focused on the supply closet itself. He stared at the gray boxes of manila envelopes on the shelves, the high stacks of neat blue books, wide flat sheets of oaktag, a dozen gradebooks bound with a thick dirty rubber band. Damn, just the thick dirty rubber band was somehow a turn-on.

Suddenly Brian's nose began to bleed. With a gesture of relief, he pulled out his handkerchief and tilted his head back in a flash, a long-practiced gesture.

"Oh, dear," Mary squeaked. "Can I help?"

"Not to worry. Gone in a minute." This counterstimulus caused Brian's erection to subside. The trickle from his nose stopped as Brian walked briskly to the men's room to wash.

Things must be really bad with me, he thought. Thank God I wasn't talking to Cherry. She'd really take revenge. At the thought of Cherry's revenge, little Scotty began to rise again.

Steve was late. He tore up the path from the parking lot, kicking gravel as he raced toward the student union. Through the heavy glass doors, the oval wall clock showed 10:00 A.M. Trotting across the empty lobby toward the elevators, he saw no colleagues. They must have started grading papers long ago. Wrong, there was mouselike Igor Blavatsky in his green tweed suit, tapping the elevator button with a jittery finger.

Although both men taught evening classes, Igor was even more obscure than Steve, an adjunct paid by the hour who hardly ever appeared in the English office in daylight. By the time Igor scurried in to get his mail, Ramona and Gloria had gone home; the only ensign of the department was Raheem, an evening student, who sat at the secretary's desk poring over his biology homework, occasionally answering the telephone.

Steve nodded at Igor without saying a word. In the past Steve had never said two words to Igor, could never get a fix on him. Whenever Steve glimpsed him creeping around the dim corridors of ESF, he always looked too subfusc and miserable to approach.

Today Igor was transformed, alert, smiling (albeit nervously), not so much like a rat who'd got into the d-Con. "Hullo," he said warmly in an exotic Russo-Brit accent. "We are both late today."

"Had a flat on the highway. Nerve-wracking. There was hardly any shoulder." Igor looked at him uncomprehendingly. How much English did he really know, anyway? Of course, he was an English teacher, but so many adjuncts were just hired at the last minute as warm bodies. They mostly taught remedial English or freshman composition, classes the professors shunned.

"The verge was very narrow," Steve added, and Igor grinned in sympathy, showing spectacularly crooked teeth.

At last the elevator doors opened. They entered together, Steve looking down at his dirty hands and the greasy smear on the front of his trousers. "Filthy job."

"You have some on your forehead." Igor pointed to his own temple, seat of comprehension, an unseemly bulge on his narrow head.

Steve groaned. "I struggled and struggled, but couldn't get the lugs off the wheel."

Igor's eyes went blank again, as if Steve were talking Hungarian.

"It's my girlfriend's car. The idiots at the garage must have tightened the nuts with a pneumatic wrench, and I only had the poor awkward thing that came with the car." Steve mimed backbreaking labor.

"The electricity in my flat finished," Igor said with a

small melancholy shrug, "and with it my alarm clock. Now we must march straight in like toy soldiers and take our places under all eyes."

"Lucille will be livid," Steve agreed.

"Lucille reminds me of a security officer I knew in Petersburg. She is on my trail always."

"But she can never remember what she said to you last time! You know, continuous total amnesia. Look, if you wait while I wash up, we can go in together and dilute the blame."

"Capital," Igor said with a shrug. "I'm willing. At this portion, not much to lose."

Table five? Table number five? To Harry Rhett's unutterable joy, he had been assigned by the vagaries of the Grade-in Committee's much-doctored quasi-alphabetical list to the very same table as the Chair. At last! His chance to shine! To show his brilliance and extreme suitability for a full-time teaching line. How often did a graduate assistant get a chance to sit next to the Chair? Never, except by a fluke of the alphabetical list.

The Chair looked lonely sitting all by himself at the head of a table for ten, his pudgy fingers nervously playing with his Mont Blanc pen, a wistful smile on his face. Harry Rhett felt like rushing over and hugging him, but then he suddenly recollected that this Chair was soon retiring, useless for the fall semester. Drat!

Instead of seating himself immediately, Harry continued to study the list to see what other senior faculty had made table number five. Whoopee! Hoo ha! He'd hit the jackpot this time. His research showed no fewer than two other full professors, Maurice el-Okdah, a black man with a big reputation, and Dickie Walter, a longtime P & B fuddy-duddy, as well as Allen Swain, a faggoty associate professor in film.

Hmm, hmm, let's see. Harry's mind was racing overtime because the list was not conveniently arranged by tables but by individual names, and his eye bounced back and forth looking for that magic digit "5." Was his best strategy to sit down next to the Chair, hoping that the other senior people would flock to that side of the long table and surround Harry with heaven-sent opportunity? But wouldn't the junior people flock first if they arrived first and wouldn't that cut Harry off from the choicest eavesdropping and the fanciest opportunities to shine?

Oh, it was a killer moment, and Harry thought not for the first time that if only he had won a Marshall fellowship or a Mellon, he wouldn't be in this difficult position. If only he hadn't started law school in error and not discovered his error till he graduated, he'd be studying English at a top-ranked place right now and he wouldn't have to be taxing his wits every moment, doubling and redoubling his ploys for advancement. If only he hadn't married his high school sweetheart, Sandy Sprouls, who was at the time the prettiest and the poorest girl in Falls

Church, Virginia, he wouldn't be wholly dependent on his wits, which were quick but not quick enough for some of these pushy New York competitors. His future would be assured. He wouldn't be at a cheap-tuition place like Muni, wondering where to sit and possibly making a fool of himself.

Meanwhile no other readers showed up to force the issue. The Chair still sat wistfully playing with his pen, but the stress of the moment was killing Harry Rhett. His hand trembled as he ticked off the names of the junior people on the list with his blue Prismalo pencil, and he pursed his rosy mouth. With his small trim body togged in good navy blue blazer and gray flannel pants, bright red tie tucked neatly into tattersall waistcoat, he felt good enough to eat.

Who were the other junior people? No real competition! Steve Speck, for example, a good-natured nerd, of no use to anyone, even himself, who dressed in ancient chinos, threadbare shirt, mile-wide tie, tweed jacket filched from some cafeteria coatrack. Well, there was Brian McGlinchee, maker of teaching schedules, a good man to know but a hard one to get close to, and Igor Blavatsky, an out-of-it outsider. Plus two women, Mary Burnson, a ditz, a worse-than-useless ditz, and Cherry Binder, fired, defiant, a downright dangerous person to know. (Here a number of stern biblical texts on the evils of women popped into Harry's mind.)

He was about to sit at a table, if you wanted to look

at it in a certain light, with a puffed-with-pride nigger, a faggot, a godless commie, a Jew (the Chair), and a dyke feminist, but if necessary he would charm the pants off all of them to nail a full-time job.

More and more colleagues were now entering the grading area, clutching their mimeographed lists, clattering their chairs as they took their seats. Neighbor leaned toward neighbor, loosening tongues, as a hum of grumbling and grousing filled the room. To Harry's ear the din sounded like a motor, chugging the department along, advancing those who deserved to advance, and dragging along the useless, too.

There! He spotted Professors el-Okdah and Walter entering the room together, absorbed in conversation. They approached table five, mouths moving vivaciously, all seamless talk. Some theoretical battle of the inkpots, no doubt. El-Okdah's last review in the *Times Book Review*, an attack on Baraka, had caused a commotion. El-Okdah had really raked Amiri over the coals. Harry chuckled to himself.

As if by reflex the two men seated themselves at the opposite end of the table from the Chair without missing a syllable of their entrancing dialogue. From his end, the Chair nodded casually. El-Okdah and Walter nodded casually back. Harry scooted in and took his seat on the left side of the table, next to el-Okdah. Nobody nodded to him, but he exulted, anyway. All he had to do was look intelligent and insert himself at the appropriate moment.

"The stool sample really frightened me," el-Okdah said. Harry looked away quickly and fixed his gaze on Walter.

"McDuff's on a low-fat diet," el-Okdah continued, "and requires lots of exercise, and you know how often I travel from conference to conference. The people my trainer recommended seem lazy and stupid. I don't even think they like animals. McDuff is always extremely manic when I return; once he hit the wall with his tail so violently there were blood spots everywhere."

"Horrible." Walter shook his head. "I couldn't trust anyone to care for Fido at home. He's a Jack Russell terrier, very loving and sensitive. Look!" Dickie glanced around, as if to see if anyone was monitoring the conversation. He seemed a bit put out to note Harry staring at him, but continued anyway. "I know this kennel in Litchfield, Connecticut, a very special place. A dog can be happy there. They don't take everyone, but I can give you their name." He scribbled a name on a scrap of pasteboard he took from his inside breast pocket. "I'm writing it on the back of the gastroenterologist's card, two birds with one stone."

"Maybe you should give me the vet's name, too. Frankly, I'm sick of endless lectures about obesity leading to kidney problems and back problems and arthritis. My dog is leading an extremely happy life. What an alarmist!"

"Amos Petty. A superb diagnostician."

Harry's eyes were beginning to glaze over. He'd

never cared for pets himself, so much babying and feeding, billing and cooing. For a long time Sandy had begged to keep a hamster at home, but he'd put his foot down. He felt the same about small children.

"Lucky to run into you," el-Okdah boomed in his rich baritone, stroking his grizzled goatee. "Looks like these grade-ins do have a function, ho ho."

At the same moment, Mary Burnson drifted over with a cup of coffee. She seated herself in the middle of the right side of the table, equidistant from the two professorial ends, glancing neither left nor right, entirely missing the Chair's benedictory nod. With furrowing brow she began reviewing Lucille's training manual to prepare herself for grading. Hopeless, thought Harry Rhett. Brain of a bird. No one else had even brought the bulky thing.

Here, too, was Allen Swain briskly seating himself alongside the Chair. "'Lo, Ed," he said. "Do I have time to make a long-distance telephone call before we start?"

"You're asking me?" the Chair replied with a shrug. "Lucille is the muck-a-muck here. She'd have us shackled to the table if she could."

"You sound dispirited."

"Am I not? Please tell me why you want to be Chair. It doesn't bring happiness, I assure you."

"Preelection depression. You're about to hand over your power to another."

"It's not so simple, Allen. Be in my shoes and you'll

soon see. And what is power? Does it excuse you from grading proficiency exams? Does it keep you from getting annoying telephone calls?"

Harry Rhett could hear each word plainly, but he couldn't understand the Chair's remark. What is power? An odd question to ask at a college function.

"Vitamin B-12 is the only answer," el-Okdah was saying.

Just as Allen Swain darted off, Brian McGlinchee, whose face had the innocent pink scrubbed look of a toddler's, appeared on the other side of the Chair. He immediately began chatting up Mary Burnson, entirely ignoring the Chair at his elbow. No hesitation at all, he knew what he wanted, pretty cool behavior for a fellow whose tenure decision had been deferred in some strange way. "You and Michelangelo!" he said meaningfully, and Mary laughed.

The din at the surrounding tables was growing louder, and Harry was having serious trouble keeping track of both ends of the table.

For some reason el-Okdah and Walter had started criticizing Cambridge, Massachusetts. Oh, that's right—they'd both attended Harvard. Not at the same time, of course. El-Okdah was probably older, but it was hard to tell with his kind, that unlined smooth skin. Couldn't be that young, but his sensationally successful book, *Griot to Grunge*, had only appeared a few years ago.

El-Okdah was shaking his grizzled head, looking

mournful. ". . . so deteriorated. Unbelievable traffic, and a highway underpass smack in front of Memorial Hall."

"All kinds of riffraff roaming Harvard Square," Walter chimed in. "A couple with a tin cup and a sign, 'Support Free Love.' Both male! Both wearing rugby jerseys! Why, the last time I was there during the Head of the Charles Regatta, you couldn't *walk* on the sidewalk without being pushed into the gutters by louts from Boston and their foul-mouthed molls."

El-Okdah nodded again. "What about those expensive yuppie cafes instead of good old Hays-Bicks?"

"Hiring women left and right . . . No jobs left for white male graduate students, even those with the best . . ." At this point el-Okdah didn't nod, but Harry did. Walter suddenly seemed to recollect himself, as a sudden loud clapping of hands broke off his complaints.

Lucille Streng, girdled up in a power suit, was standing at the center table clapping for everyone's attention.

"Now, now," she was saying. "Socializing's over. Save it for the party. We have serious work ahead of us. I want to begin training you, and I must have everyone's attention. You, too, Quinton. I see you over there. I have my eye on you. Cut the comedy and let's get to it.

"For those of you who've never graded proficiency exams before, it requires the finest discrimination in order to make the program a success. Essays are graded on a scale of one to five. Your training booklet contains one essay for each category, and I'm sure you've studied this material diligently, but let's go over it again one more time to reinforce our common standards. In brief, a five paper means that the writer is so good he doesn't have to take English 1 but can pass directly to English 2. That means he's eloquent. I mean eloquent, well-organized, uses language fluently, can use metaphors to make his point, and can handle complex sentences. We all are looking for students like this, but that doesn't mean we're going to find any."

Tittering went up from the surrounding tables.

"A four, on the other hand, is your good English 1 student. He needs language work, but is able to organize a paragraph around a topic sentence and make a general point. A three will also go to English 1, but he's got problems in punctuation that need to be addressed, and he's wordy, rambling, uses too many words to make his point and goes roundabout. You know the type.

"Now the two, he's got basic trouble organizing his ideas, and he makes very serious punctuation mistakes. He's never going to pass English 1 so send him to remedial English and see that he goes straight."

More tittering. At this moment Allen Swain was walking back to table five from his telephone conversation. It must have been a successful call, for he was smiling, and as he threaded his precise way among the tables filled with his colleagues, it almost looked as though the department was tittering at him, and he was accepting their laughter with thanks.

"One is barely coherent. You're not going to have much trouble identifying him. The most troublesome are the twos and threes, and all the borderlines. Then we have the separate problem of foreign students. Grouping these folks are not your problem. They should have been weeded out at the exam. If, however, an English-as-a-second-language student has found their way by mistake into your pile, that is to say if it doesn't sound like English but it sounds like a non-English speaker, why then, walk over to Carole-Ann Henderson-Lerner, she's sitting by the door. Stand up, Carole-Ann, and let us see you." A little red-headed woman in a yellow pullover stood up. "Carole-Ann is our ESL liaison. She will accept foreign essays and she will help you identify them if you are in doubt. Just walk over there with them, okay? Good. You can sit down, Carole-Ann.

"Now we're going to test your mettle on this. Betsy will pass out some sample essays, and I'm going to ask you to read them and assess them, and then raise your hand so we can get some kind of departmental consensus."

This part of the grade-in always sent chills up Harry's spine. What if you were the *only* one to raise your hand and it turned out that everyone else in the department, yes, *everyone*, disagreed with your opinion? Harry hated to be wrong in any case, but to be wholly publicly wrong was a nightmare.

The first essay didn't look inviting. It looked like a failing paper to Harry. But what if he were wrong?

"My Inner Self"

If I really knew myself I would not reconize mysef. What I do and say are what I want people to think I am, not the real me. I am afraid to bring out what I really am. If I act and did what I really want to do, people will say I am crazy. I like to play in the street just like a little boy does. I would like to run barefoot thru the street having the sidewalk warm my feet in the summer and cool them in the winter. To let loose and do what I always want to do, that is being my true self. I don't want to pretend that I am some else. I act like my friends act, I smoke because they smoke, I drink because they drink. I just want to do what I like to do. I don't like to smoke and drink, but I do it because my friend do it. If I don't smoke and drink, I would have no friend. Everywhere I go or anyone I meet, I have to act differenly everytime according to the friend I have. If they curse, I have to curse, If they rob, I have to rob. I can't act like myself I say act because everyone act out 1 part in life, know matter who she or he may be, every-one act out a part in life. Know one brings

out his true self. Maybe they are afraid to show people what they really are. Someone who is weak, will
act like a bully, someone who is scare, will act brave.
You don't have to be an actor or actress to act out a
part in life. I just act to have friend. I am frighten of
being alone. For by being my true self my friends
would not know me and will not want to know me.
If I had to act tuff, I would do it, if I had to act meek,
I would do it. I will act anyway I could to get friend.

Harry's mind started to go into overdrive. He looked
around the table. Most of his colleagues had finished
reading the essay and were looking around with a calm
self-satisfied air. The Chair was still bending over the
paper, his large brow wrinkling. If Harry didn't know better, he'd think the Chair was moving his lips.

"Okay, folks," Lucille cried out in a happy voice.
"You've had way enough time to consider this paper. How
many among you would consider this a five?"

Heads were swivelling. Not a single hand was raised.
Of course! The essay was riddled with errors. But it was so
easy to get rattled, and in panic just throw up your hand
to release your tension.

In a slyer voice, Lucille asked, "How many of you
think this is a four?"

One hand was raised. Quinton Bloch. He looked
around at everyone looking at him. "Good essay," he
boomed. "Completely honest, rare in student work."

"Honesty is not one of our criterions," Lucille said in a severe tone.

Quinton laughed and shrugged. Okay for Quinton to be blasé, thought Harry. He was starting a new life at NYU next term.

"Tell me now, people." Lucille's voice was teasing, cunning, false. "Is this a three?"

Harry ran over the faults quickly. No paragraphing whatsoever, no clear development, numerous spelling errors. But paragraphing was a fairly easy error to correct. On the other hand, just as Quinton said, the writer was sincere, you could almost say eloquent. That bit about his foot feeling the heat of the sidewalk, that was good. "If they curse, I have to curse," that was good, too. This guy had brains and with some guidance could pass English 1.

Other hands had gone up, quite a few other hands, and Harry's hand was sort of itching to go up there with them, but by now it was too late. His tardy response would be noticed. Lucille began counting, "Thirteen . . . no, fourteen for number three."

"And how many for number two?" and there was just a little emphasis in Lucille's voice that made Harry think it must be two so he threw up his hand and with a great burst of relief saw that lots of other hands all around him had flown up in the air as well. He was in the majority, the blessed majority.

"And number one?"

A sprinkling of hands, that of the Chair among

them. He was muttering, "Illiterate. Shocking. Glad I'm retiring, getting out of here."

Lucille threw up her meaty arms in the gesture of a referee after a countdown. "Well, folks, you've got the idea. This is a clear number two. It's just not good enough to be anything else, get it? This should be your number two."

At this moment Harry felt a disturbance on the edges of the crowd, and two figures, one tall and one short, began to scuttle among the tables, looking neither right nor left. Who should it be but Steve Speck and Igor Blavatsky?

Harry allowed a knowing smile to linger on his lips. The worst thing in the world they could do—arrive late to this affair and miss the important training and have Lucille's cold eyes rest upon them, along with the thousand eyes of the whole department. Some people are born to succeed and some are born to fail. "Everyone act out a part in life," as Writer Two so sagely said, and Speck and Blavatsky were acting the part of idiots. They didn't deserve to be English teachers, that's for sure.

8

By noon the tall piles of blue books on the grading tables had shrunk. To make up for their late arrival, Steve and Igor worked without lifting their heads. All around them on the top floor of the student union, the suffering faculty groaned and whispered.

Why am I forced to do this? I loved Dorothea in Middlemarch, *my only sin; why am I punished?*

"I would that we were, my beloved, white birds on the foam of the sea!"

Why do I have to grade when I have menstrual cramps?

These illiterate bastards don't deserve a college education.

"I'm going to talk to that Carole-Ann," Brian said, pushing himself away from the table as from the dissecting table in the morgue, a gray look on his once ruddy face. "I don't know *what* I've got here, it's not English, maybe Indo-European."

Mary barely nodded, her attention engaged on her fortieth "My Inner Self."

"Will you be quiet," the Chair said testily. "I'm trying to concentrate on these blasted things." His stack was still enormous.

How quickly the Chair grows senile, Dickie Walter thought.

I am wiser than these students, Harry Rhett thought.

I should be paid more, Allen Swain thought.

I should have stayed at Oxford, though the climate was vile, Murray el-Okdah thought. *"I went far wrong."*

A tall thin man in a blue windbreaker, carrying a maroon knapsack, slipped into the grading area and moved straight to table five. He sat down in Brian's vacant seat and after removing two pens from a zippered compartment began reading the top blue book in Brian's pile. Mary, engrossed, paid little notice, but when she shifted slightly in her chair she saw that the shape beside her had elongated.

"George Reilly, what are you doing here?" she squealed.

"My bit," he replied. "Why so surprised?"

"Aren't you on disability leave?"

"I am, but why should I shirk my responsibility? I can grade as well as the next man."

In a few minutes, a little ripple of recognition ran through the room. Soon the whole department was staring at George, who hadn't been seen in public since Lauren's memorial service.

"Oh, God!" said Lucille from the other side of the room, holding her head in her hands. "What's he going to do next? Give another eulogy?" With George anything was possible. And what if that maroon knapsack held an assault rifle?

Well, it's not my headache any more, the Chair and Quinton thought simultaneously.

Brian, returning to his seat, did a double take, but, recognizing an opportunity for departmental service, took the vacant chair next to George. "You're sitting in my seat, George, reading my blue books," he said quietly. "Are you okay?"

"Why is everyone so concerned with my welfare? I'm fulfilling my responsibility, bothering no one. Do I seem so cock-a-hoop?"

"No," said Brian, realizing that George spoke the truth. "Give me back a few exams. You can be my second reader."

As George bent his head to his work, Brian made a shaking motion with his hand behind his back, meaning, Let him be.

So George was left alone while the exhausting work went on.

Lucille didn't have time to hang around and keep an eye on George. Because the annual party was being held across the floor in the Flushing Room, Lucille had to keep running back and forth to oversee arrangements. She was in charge of catering as she was in charge of so many other things, large and small, things no one else really wanted to do.

Who, for example, would remember that refreshment tables required elegant departmental tablecloths with a sturdy plastic departmental liner underneath? That because of missing ice buckets, white wine must be refrigerated downstairs until the last minute? That hard cheese required hard-cheese cutters? It was difficult to imagine Quinton negotiating patiently with the commissary staff over the hors d'oeuvres, or Murray el-Okdah washing musty-looking pâté knives in the men's room sink.

With Betsy's help, Lucille arranged the spoons and paper napkins to her satisfaction. Then the food she'd ordered was carried in on the usual large metal trays. But instead of the little sandwiches of shrimp salad, cucumber, and brie, or smoked tongue with carrot curls and luscious petits fours, the commissary had sent trays full of baloney, peanut butter and jelly, and dry graham crackers.

"Are you mad?" Lucille shouted at the carrier, Gabriel, a short, perplexed Hispanic man. "This is our sole departmental function for the year! Unacceptable!"

"We have nothing else," Gabriel replied. "Deliveries cancelled. Budget problems."

I've gone down, down, down, Lucille thought. At her first faculty appointment, Bryn Mawr in the sixties, the departmental table boasted a silver tea service, cream-filled ladyfingers, hand-baked Toll House cookies, chocolate-dipped apricots. But they didn't want her at Bryn Mawr, despite her backbreaking labor, long hours in the library, extra committee assignments. They didn't want her. After twenty years, it still rankled.

Her appointment at Muni proved equally unrewarding. Senior male faculty taught most of the desirable courses. As soon as Lucille's novel course started being offered every other semester, the handwriting was on the wall here, too. She retrained, developed an interest in remedial writing, became indispensable running whatever program nobody else cared about. I'll never retire, never, she'd sworn so often, but this miserable peanut butter spread had brought her as close as she'd ever been to that dire eventuality.

"Tell your boss to come up here and look me in the eye," she blustered. "Does he really think I'll take this lying down? And what about the bartender they promised?" She looked at Gabriel dubiously. "Are you the one who's tending bar?"

"I got to go back."

"You mean they're not sending us a bartender?"

The man shook his head.

"Oh, God. Betsy—quick. Go call Harry Rhett. I don't care if he's still grading. He's got to be bartender. And he needs to get an apron and a rag for the bar. Go tell him to get down to the cafeteria and they'll fix him up. Don't let him give you an argument about being too high and mighty. I don't care how high his GRE scores were. He's our bartender. He'll be good at it, too. I'm going to the deli to buy some decent food. I'll charge it to the college and to hell with who pays for it."

"Can't wait for those party dainties," George said as he flipped the last blue book onto Brian's pile.

"Shouldn't you go home and take it easy?" Mary asked, though she secretly hoped that George would stay and flirt with her a little. Though noticeably older-looking than he was last fall, his cheeks hollowed, the forelock of black hair now streaked with strands of silver, George still made her heart beat fast.

"Nonsense, I'm just getting warmed up. Haven't been to a party in a long time, not that these affairs can be called parties, too stiff, more like job interviews or PTA functions."

Brian and Mary exchanged glances.

"I see my friend the distinguished poet across the way is also finishing. Congratulations, Igor Blavatsky," George called in a hearty voice across the grading table. "I hear you just won the Folondelli Prize."

Igor raised his pale face from his papers and blushed to the tip of his freckled nose.

"Is that so?" said Brian, who had never exchanged a word with Igor and had never heard of the Folondelli

Prize. "A prestigious award?" He looked searchingly across the table at the little ratlike man.

"I'm in topping good mood today," Igor said, showing all his crooked teeth in a delighted grin. "Big cash prize, including trip to Rome."

"*The Wolf Pine Plateau* is a superb, marvelous sequence," George explained. "Igor is the Russian Yeats. I'm the one who recommended him for the job, but this is the first time I've run into him. Let's go and drink to his health."

"Off-campus," Brian said urgently. "Drink off-campus."

"And miss an exciting department meeting? Not on your life. C'mon, Igor. Let's go across and guzzle. You come, too, Mary," George said as an afterthought. "And Brian as well. But they won't have any vodka. I know a Greek nightclub nearby we can go to after, with Metaxa and a belly dancer."

As the blue books were finally being collected and hauled away, the men and women of the English department felt punchy; they were reeling and they hadn't even had a drink yet. In an untidy mob they crossed the floor to the Flushing Room and engulfed the food supply. Standing in clusters and gripping their red or white wine and their Sausalito cookies and cotto salami on sesame rye and whatever else Lucille had scraped up at the corner deli, they gobbled and gabbled. They circulated but not too widely, a foot or two to the right or left as if they were dancing.

Steve was the last to leave his grading table, delayed by an adjudication. Occasionally a blue book needed a third grade because the first and second readers disagreed so violently. Quinton had awarded Shawna Powell's essay a five, but the Chair had given her a one, with the comment "obvious plagiarism." Shawna was a poet with a dazzling style a little better than Steve's, but even if she was a plagiarist, how did she know that the topic was going to be "My Inner Self"?

As Steve puzzled, the room emptied out, and Heidi, the collector, wanted him to finish quickly so she could join the party, too. "Don't make such a production of it," she urged.

"I don't know. I don't know," he agonized. He could put a four on the exam and make some teacher of English 1 very happy to have Shawna in the class, but why penalize Shawna for being gifted and eloquent? To hell with it, he thought finally, and put a bold five on the cover. I hope I'm not making a damn fool of myself. And now I have no one to go into the party with!

Daphne and Dickie were also late in reaching the party, having taken loads of time to primp in their respective rest rooms.

"Shouldn't the party be coming *after* the election?

Wouldn't that be more logical?" Dickie complained for the fifth time. "Isn't it more fun that way?"

"By tradition the party comes *before*," Daphne said. "That's how you persuade your voters. Collecting votes, that's the true fun."

They quickened their pace as they heard the roar of voices from the Flushing Room. "Everyone will be too flushed with drink to vote correctly," Dickie said in a worried voice. "Daphne—I told you this wasn't a good idea."

"I do love a party!" Daphne purred, ignoring Dickie's worries as she always did. Daphne enjoyed parties because she believed that *she* was the soul of the party, attractive, magnetic. She adored wandering from cluster to cluster, exchanging clever, sparkling phrases.

Now she moved across the floor in a little bubble of elation. She'd shopped for days for her café au lait trapeze dress that swooped behind her slender body like a sail. She had a becoming new hairstyle. She was going to be Chair. In the future the department would do exactly what she wished. Daphne envisioned progress forms, printed forms to cover every contingency: attendance, papers, conferences, the works! Not time consuming, no. Each professor would merely check off a box or two each week for each class and sign his name and rank in pen, not pencil. An Oversight Committee would oversee the forms. And Daphne would oversee the Oversight Committee. Intoxicating!

Just inside the room she saw that beautiful young man with the funny name standing awkwardly by himself, a wallflower. Swanlike neck, masses of raven black hair, downcast eyes, mile-long lashes, but there was something so odd about him. He was undoubtedly clever, his academic credentials superior, but he seemed . . . oblivious. Oblivious of what, his good looks? His social obligations? She didn't quite know.

"Do get me a drink, Dickie, like a dear," she said, steering a course towards . . . what was his name?

"Your first time grading?" she asked, dropping anchor at his side with a Bette Davis–like shuttle of her hips.

"Oh, no, Professor Pryce-Jones, I was here last year."

Steve felt abashed. Daphne had been so mean-spirited at his interview, poking fun at Henry Martin and at him, and here she was radiating charm. Was it his vote she wanted? He was bound to Allen, who'd been kind to him. She should realize that.

"And you're planning to be here next year?"

"If you'll have me."

Daphne smiled benevolently. "If it were up to me . . . of course. But budget is queen here. A Columbia Ph.D. should have no difficulty finding an appointment elsewhere."

"That's not what I've heard." Daphne was staring at him with such a funny look on her face, as if she were choosing a Crunchie Bar from a sweets counter.

"Have you investigated jobs in ESL?"

"I've no training in ESL. My field is modern poetry."

"Oh, that—" she said, swooping out her hand and almost whacking Dickie, who was approaching with two drinks in his hands.

"Dickie, you know our friend . . . Seth."

"Steve. Steve Speck."

"We're talking over his possibilities for next year."

Dickie refused to be drawn into this boring topic. "I often think of the question Borges asked me when he was seated next to me at a luncheon at the Harvard Club. His food had been cut up for him, but since he couldn't see what he was eating, a lot was flapping around on the front of his face. He turned to me and said, 'And what do *you* do *exactly*?' I was so paralyzed I couldn't remember what I did."

Steve and Daphne laughed insincerely.

Steve thought, Is Daphne really showing a preference for me? Why do these bizarre things happen?

During a lull, Allen came walking up to the bar where Harry Rhett drooped. A large white apron shielded Harry's good gray pants, its longish strings wrapped twice around his waist and tied in front. He'd removed his tattersall waistcoat and red tie and rolled up his shirtsleeves.

"Any sherry?"

"You must be joking," Harry replied belligerently. "Cheap red or cheap white, that's the lot."

"How'd you get this job?" Allen asked as Harry handed over his plastic wineglass with a trembling hand. "You were grading at my table just a minute ago, weren't you?"

"Oh, you noticed? Yes, I got this job because I'm the blottom of the ladder, that's why. *Bot*tom of the ladder, I mean. Smelly graduate assistant. What choice do I have?"

"Well, cheer up—" Allen made a toasting motion. "Here's to better days."

Harry shivered. "I'm a minister's son or I'd tell you where to stuff it."

Allen chuckled. "You're bitter, but believe me, if you've landed an assistantship in these hard times, you must be talented. I'm an expert in the career advancement line."

"Then how is it you're only an asshole professor, pardon me, associate professor?"

"Touché. I see your blood is up. But you're too quickly carried away by your righteous feelings. Why offend unnecessarily? Go easy, walk gently. Never drink on duty."

"Stuff your advice," Harry said, pushing out his rosy red lips. "*I* have no vote in the election, in case you've forgotten."

"Childish. Ill advised. Five more minutes and you'll destroy your career. Chill out." Allen began to move away, then turned back to Harry and said, "Nonetheless, if you want a career, come around to my office on Monday after my last class and I'll plan your advancement."

Harry made a noncommittal murmur in his throat as he watched Allen's boyish back departing through the crowd, but before he poured his next drink, he paused and reached for the seltzer instead of the wine. "Some have entertained angels unawares . . . ," he thought blasphemously.

Aimee grew tired of waiting in Steve's office, which in its cold clamminess felt like a detention cell. Her needlework bored her. To pass the time she went through Steve's desk drawers, looking for love letters or incriminating photographs, but all she found were unclaimed student themes, faded mimeographed poems, and some brittle honey menthol cough drops.

A rich man's daughter, she was used to doing just as she liked, so she walked across the quad and entered the forbidding lobby of the student union, asked where the English party was, and went on up. Steve had not forbidden her to crash the departmental party because he'd never dreamed she would try.

Unimpaired by career ambitions, Aimee sauntered through the doorway of the Flushing Room, smiling in a friendly way. Wearing her usual Pre-Raphaelite costume of lawny white dress and a leghorn hat with a purple streamer down the back above her flowing dark hair, she caused a sensation with the wine-befuddled male faculty. Having spent all morning pondering the desiccated inner self, they were only too happy to gaze at Aimee's young and beautiful outer self. They abandoned the dowdy female graduate assistants. No real man would dream of flirting with Heidi Weismuller in her navy blue blazer that reeked of the orphanage.

Aimee smiled at George Reilly, whose splendid head was the first she encountered. "Can you direct me to Steve Speck?"

"No spouses!" Lucille rushed forward on powerful legs, but George laid his hand upon Aimee's arm.

George was feeling fine. Such a long time since he'd been to a party. His brother's house had been more like a penitentiary. A rock garden of boulders and cacti outside the sliding door, but he wasn't allowed to walk there in the daylight. Georgia (as his brother's wife was so annoyingly called) requested that he keep the blinds shut. A bloody tomb. And the neighbors, golfers with metallic voices. So he'd just packed his underwear and left, though he'd promised to stay till the end of the term. No harm done, his Arizona adventure, except to his cats who'd run off, poor Absalom and Achitophel.

Yes, George had decided to seek pleasure and forget what was troubling him. Only in the middle of the night did he sometimes remember. A professional cleaning service, Maids of New York—three burly men—cleaned out his apartment. They dealt with the old flower pots and wire hangers, dead flashlight batteries and ancient roach motels. At his request they'd removed all letters, photographs, postcards with their disturbing messages. By now he couldn't recall what they said. His apartment was bare and soothing. There wasn't even much dust on the books.

"This party needs some bazouki music," he was telling Igor, his feet jiggling to unheard rhythms, when he saw the girl come through the door in a white dress from a dream, her long dark hair unbound under a straw hat. She couldn't be more than seventeen, but with lascivious promise in her gait. He laid his hand on her arm and she looked at him with more promise.

"I'm Steve Speck's girlfriend." Aimee smiled. She had the slight suggestion of an overbite so rare in wealthy girls.

"I respect Steve," George replied, "but I think we should talk."

They took the elevator down to the third floor and walked around in the dark empty corridors as though it were a conservatory garden. George talked to Aimee in a sweet chirping voice as if charming birds. "I can't tell you what an impression you made on me as you walked through the door. I realized for the first time that death needn't put an end to love. When you've been wounded the way I have . . ."

Aimee listened in silence and leaned on his arm.

"Let me give you my telephone number," he said at the end. "I won't pursue you any more than this. I've learned my lesson about women, but if you should decide to leave Steve and come and live with me . . ."

"What a romantic you are!" she said, looking pleased.

"Where's George?" Mary asked Brian, when she returned from the ladies', a long trek almost to Nassau County.

"He left with a young woman," Brian said, smirking. "That guy is really something. I doubt he knows his own name at this point, but he still has an eye for a sexy girl."

"Are you joking? You let him walk off with a girl? How do you know what he'll do? You know he's . . . not himself."

"He's himself, all right. What my dad used to call a true bullshit artist. But the funny thing is, he hardly said anything to her . . ."

Mary was drooping, looking pained, her love for George like a rope burn. "It's hard to see where this is all going to end."

"It's going to end in an election," Brian answered, for he'd caught sight of Daphne and Lucille charging the room from two opposite ends like well-trained sheepdogs.

"Department meeting at two o'clock in Humanities 17A," they were barking in unison.

"Why would you stay?" Steve was saying to Igor in the opposite corner. "You don't even have a vote."

"Is for me exotic experience. To push nose where it doesn't belong is poet's responsibility."

"I guess you're right about poets, but elections here at Muni are pretty boring. For example, I don't think our insurgent can win. His base is small, mostly junior people."

"But that female"—Igor pointed to Daphne, who was herding an elderly faculty member with curt remarks and little butts on the elbow—"is from Shakespeare, 'from the neck down they are sea serpents,' or such like. *King Lear*. Why would *she* be elected?"

"Well, Daphne's been on the P & B forever, and she gets elected time after time." Steve scratched his head in puzzlement. One glass of white wine could make him dopey. "I guess they think she's experienced, knows the ropes. Can stand up to the administration, too, that's what a chair's supposed to do. Stands up for us, so must be tough. Why a sea serpent, I don't know." He scratched his head again. "There are a few nice people in the department, but they don't get involved in politics. Nice guys don't run, you understand?"

"Best lack all conviction, worst full of passionate intensity," Igor muttered in his heavy accent. "I quote from the Irish Blavatsky, hah, hah!"

"Down from the waist they are centaurs," Steve said suddenly. "That's what you meant. But it's very fine you've read some Shakespeare. I must say I'm weak in Pushkin and Lermontov and those fellows."

A mocking laugh sounded immediately behind them. "Weak in Lermontov?" George shrilled. "If I were Chair, I'd make Russian mandatory for English majors. Chinese as well. Mandatory!"

George's eyes were glittering. "In fact, my own special course, one I'd teach myself . . . but keep it to yourself, Daphne mustn't hear about this. She loves to thwart me." George looked around suspiciously. "Well, I'll tell you, it's sensational. Never been done before! Literature of the Aliens!"

"You mean immigrant lit?" Steve inquired helpfully. "African tales, Hispanic and Irish and Jewish myths?"

"No, no, no. Of the *Aliens*. Communications from other realms. You know what I mean."

Steve and Igor exchanged glances.

"By the way, Steve, my boy, I have a communication from your lovely companion." George pulled a note from his shirt pocket. "She's angry with you. I hope nothing's wrong."

"You mean from Aimee?"

"To be sure."

"How'd you get it? Was she over here?"

"Indeed. She sounded angry. She couldn't reach you. I was sympathetic!"

Steve read the note—"Gone back to Manhattan

with car. See you later"—then held his head. "Oh, boy! Now I'll have to find a ride home. Maybe Cherry will show up. Why did Aimee give the note to *you*? Why didn't she tell *me*?"

But George had turned and was whispering to Igor.

By twos and threes the department was moving over to Humanities Building, metamorphosing from party to business. Mary walked across the quad weeping into her cocktail napkin, but nobody chose to notice. With bustle and loud laughter the partygoers entered 17A and took their seats in the largest classroom on campus, a chemistry lecture hall with two hundred seats, a deep amphitheater with a sink and running water on the platform at the bottom. So many cheerful faces had never been seen before in Humanities 17A. Below, the Chair was already setting out his papers on the lectern, eager to preside. Quinton was by his side.

"This is so exciting," said Heidi Weismuller. "Do you think Daphne will win?"

The graduate assistants, who had no vote, sat in a clump high up near the door, ready for easy getaway (all but Harry Rhett, who'd gone home in a huff). They peered down at the action as if at the ancient stage where gods and mortals stalked.

As election overseer, Lucille was supposed to be standing at the door handing out ballots and checking off names on the list, but because of her catering duties she arrived late. She'd stopped at Temp 6 to pick up the ballots disguised as a box of number nine envelopes under lock and key in the bottom drawer of Ramona's desk.

Ramona made a face when she handed the box over to Lucille. Security was tight, but who, after all, was checking the checker? "Make sure you don't put these in the wrong hands," she admonished. Lucille had flushed then and remained flushed, her blonde hair crisping up in exclamatory tendrils around her face.

"I think Lucille is going to have a stroke," Steve whispered to Igor, noting her red face and labored breathing as she pounded up and down the aisles handing out ballots to the already seated eligibles. Beneath her power suit a frothy pink slip showed two or three inches as she stretched across the aisle a few rows below them to hand a ballot to Maurice el-Okdah.

"She looks like Bride of Frankenstein." Steve was feeling loose, unlike himself. I'm having fun, he thought. I feel like an observer and not part of the department at all. That's just it, his gloomy sensible self reminded him. Not part of the department at all.

"Oh, look!" There was Cherry grimacing in the doorway like the evil fairy Carabosse who arrives in a coach drawn by cockroaches. With a venomous grin she began stomping down the steep amphitheater steps in her army boots.

"Over here!" Steve began waving his arms, eager to get Cherry in the seat next to him and his ride home settled at the same time. Suddenly he caught sight of Cherry's face and recalled Cherry's grievance against the department. He stopped waving.

Cherry plunked herself heavily in the very first row just behind the railing that protected the administration from the mob, ready to pronounce her curse.

Quinton and Cherry stared at each other across the railing for a long moment. Then Quinton stepped to the microphone. "Testing. One. Two. Three. While Professor Streng continues to hand out ballots, I'll begin the meeting. Does anyone want to make a motion to waive the reading of minutes of the last meeting?"

Alf Bjornsen, pale and still under heavy painkillers, had left his nursing home to cast his vote. He stood shakily and received a little pattering of applause. "I move we waive the reading of minutes," he said in solemn tones.

"Second," chimed Brian, whose regular duty this was.

"All in favor?"

"Mumbbb," went the crowd in great good humor.

"So it is. Now for some news since the previous meeting. I'm delighted to announce that Professor Georgia Fatwood, the feminist critic, will join the department in September for a one-year professorship. I'm sure you're all familiar with her scholarly work. She will teach

Feminist Novel and Women's Studies I," said Quinton, looking straight at Cherry.

Cherry sat motionless in her chair, her teeth bared in a frozen smile. Fatwood, a hack feminist with an undeserved reputation, would be teaching the courses Cherry herself had designed. Cherry, in her year of grace, would be teaching Freshman Composition! And, of course, there went the chief argument of her union grievance, that the department was prejudiced against feminists. Against her will a clicking noise sounded in Cherry's throat.

A moment or two later, Allen pattered down the steps from his perch on the aisle and seated himself next to Cherry. In full view of his colleagues he pressed Cherry's hand in commiseration, and Cherry let him.

From this point, events took over the meeting with lightning speed.

With many puffed-up words of praise, Brian nominated Daphne for Chair, seconded by Dickie Walter.

Then Cherry, fueled by a new surge of hate, made a fiery speech in favor of Allen. Blushing, Steve seconded it.

All this, pro forma. "Other nominations?" Quinton intoned. To everyone's amazement Mary Burnson slowly rose from her place midway up the aisle, where she'd been sitting hunched over, biting her forefinger.

"I think the time has come for innovative thinking. We need someone who'll take a bold new initiative, someone with vision."

Almost everyone in the assembly muttered at this idea. In the English department at Muni College, who would possibly fit this description?

"I nominate George Reilly," Mary continued.

"Professor Burnson," the Chair said sternly, pushing Quinton out of the way to get to the microphone. "Is Professor Reilly here? Only the physically present may be nominated without written affidavit."

George was sitting inconspicuously reading his Bible in a clump of people on the left side near the wall. He rose, a slim, upright figure.

"Yes, I'm willing to serve, more than happy. Be glad to give each voter a preview of my plan for the department as soon as I can have it reproduced. I've been having trouble getting copies. Dragging their feet a little, hmm." He gave the Chair a mild glance of reproach.

"Just one minute," the Chair said, even more sternly. "You may not speak in your own favor on the floor until the nomination has been duly seconded."

A long pause. George sat down. The graduate assistants in their perch near the door squirmed with excitement. "If only I'd brought my camcorder," Heidi said.

Where he sat, a few places from Daphne on one side, Mary on the other, Brian felt a powerful surge of joy. A rogue nomination. How wonderful. He wouldn't have to vote for Daphne, he'd vote for George. Secret ballot. She'd never know. But even if she did know . . . Brian's mind began to race. Wouldn't that be a wonderful thing? He'd be free to . . . work for the telephone company, manage a carpet-cleaning outfit. Would that be so terrible? What would be so terrible about that? He saw himself in front of a huge console, many flickering blue and yellow lights.

He stood, ignoring Daphne's astonished face. "I second that nomination," he cried.

Daphne popped up, glaring. "Point of order, Professor Chair. May a nominator make a second nomination? Is this valid?"

"Good point," responded the Chair. "We don't have a copy of *Robert's Rules* here, but ex cathedra let me rule this nomination invalid."

George stood up again. "Arcane point," he said. "Beneath contempt."

"I'm thrilled to pieces," Betsy Fuller whispered to Heidi, clutching her arm. "Can this be happening?"

"Sorry, George," Quinton said kindly. "You haven't been legally nominated, you see. You're an ex-nominee. Why don't you go home and rest?"

"I second Professor Reilly's nomination," a voice boomed out. With popping eyes and craning necks, everyone turned to stare at Maurice el-Okdah, who stared back without expression.

"Why is he doing this?" Cherry asked Allen, who had an alien, thunderstruck look on his face. It was rare to see Allen out of his depth.

"Haven't a clue," Allen whispered back harshly. "I know he wasn't my supporter, but I thought Daphne had him wrapped up."

"What's his motive?" Brian asked Mary, all agog.

"Why do you always have to know about motives?" Mary snapped. "Don't you trust your heart?"

Brian put his palm on his chest. Did a heart still beat? He felt joyous. He must be sick.

"Thank you for your confidence." George stood again and bowed in the general direction of el-Okdah. "I'd like to say a few words about what's wrong with this department."

Daphne popped up again like a piston. "Point of order!" she shrilled. "Nominees are allowed to circulate position papers only during election period. It's too late to hear Reilly's platform."

"That's not precisely a point of order," the Chair mused, as if to himself.

"But you never presented *any* platform, Daphne," Mary cried.

"Let them all present their platforms!" an anonymous voice called out.

"We'll be here all year!" another voice yelled.

"Been here since ten A.M.!" Another desperate scream.

"Are you trying to throttle dissent?"

"Give them a one-minute limit."

"Yes, give them one minute."

The Chair shook his head. "Members of the department—you're turning into an unruly mob. Please wait to be recognized. Professor Bjornsen?"

"I move that each candidate give us his views in one minute."

"Seconded!" ten voices cried.

"Who is doing the seconding?"

"I am," said Brian, a big smile on his face.

Dickie Walter rose to his feet, wagging his well-barbered head. "Members of the department, have you ever heard of a real academic debate that limited itself to one minute? I ask my colleagues, are we on television? Are these, what you call 'em, 'soundbites'? I make a counter-motion. Let us adjourn and meet again with cooler heads next week and have a true academic debate."

"Second the motion," Daphne and Allen cried together.

"We will have a vote on Professor Walter's motion. All in favor?"

Three tinny voices rang out.

"Against?"

A roar resounded through Humanities 17A.

"A vote in favor of Professor Bjornsen's one-minute speeches. In favor?"

A louder roar.

Dickie whispered into Daphne's ear. "I told you we shouldn't serve alcohol before the election."

"Go piss yourself."

"Professor Reilly, will you speak for one minute only?"

George smiled, shook his dark hair out of his eyes, and clasped his hands in front of him in a choirboy's posture. "In one minute I can't say much, so I'll pick one very important point, important to everybody. How long must we go on using that stupid ditto machine? When I tell my friends at other schools that I have to cut a ditto every time I want copies, they look at me as if I'm insane. Mimeographs went out in the early sixties. Why should we suffer this medieval torture? The department does own a photocopy machine, but only Ramona and the top brass . . ."

"Sounds like a rock group," Cherry whispered to Allen, but he shrugged off her comment with an angry twist of his shoulders.

". . . are allowed to use it. They've put that photocopy machine under lock and key! Other places have five or six copiers." George's bright eyes shone. A glint of spittle flecked his lips. "My platform is—let each and every member of the department have access to the copier for half an hour a week. That would be fair and practical . . . Don't worry, I worked out my figures with a calculator and everybody will . . ."

"Time's up," snapped the Chair. "Professor Swain."

Allen seemed shaken, shrunken. His scratchy voice

lacked its usual suavity. "I'd just like to say that Professor Reilly has no administrative experience. If it's a new leader you want, you'll find that I possess the necessary skills and I am also—how shall I say this?—a very stable member of the department. I know that photocopiers are budget items, and budget lines can't be switched around that easily."

Allen came to a halt and stared out at the assembly for a very long time. "I was coordinator of the Film Society of Queens, a position requiring good interpersonal skills. Last year I was voted Teacher of the Year." Another long pause.

"A new openness," Cherry whispered at his elbow.

"I will endeavor to bring a new openness to the department."

"Flexibility," Cherry whispered.

Allen shook his head. Addison DeWitt wouldn't be delivering *these* lines. That was the trouble.

"Innovation."

Allen swatted at the air in front of him in an alarming gesture. "I will be specially attentive to the needs of the younger department members and . . . ur . . . I will create a departmental ombudsman to deal with complaints and redress any wrongs."

Allen sat down abruptly, looking shell-shocked, more like George Bailey in *It's a Wonderful Life* than Addison DeWitt in *All About Eve*.

Without being prompted, Daphne rose and cleared her throat. "I will be brief. Others have spoken frankly, and I will speak equally frankly. Do you want a madman or a charlatan running the department and dealing with the administration? Do you want to get your throats cut by the president's office? If you do, vote for my opponents. Do you want to be teaching four or five days a week instead of your present two- or three-day teaching loads? Vote for my opponents! Do you want supposedly innovative programs that will bring the department to ruin? Vote for my opponents. Vote for me and I guarantee that the department will run efficiently just as it always has, without any change whatsoever." She glanced at her watch. "According to my stopwatch, this has been a half-minute speech." Daphne sat down, very pleased with herself.

The Chair looked dazed. So many pithy words had never flown by so fast in a department meeting. "Excellent, excellent. Few other departments could sustain such a worthy debate. Now, I feel, since we have been here many long hours, we must proceed with the election without further ado. Has everyone received his ballot?"

"Yes." Lucille, exhausted, sat back in her chair with her heavy limbs thrust out in front of her. "Yes, yes, yes."

"Please mark your choice. Will the Election Committee then step forward to collect and tally the ballots."

The actual vote took only a few minutes, and the

counting not much longer. When Rick Clodfelder, chairman of the Elections Committee, stepped forward to announce the results, a hush like that of a final exam filled Humanities 17A. "The new chair is Professor Reilly!"

"Yahooo!" George leaped to his feet with a great cowboy cheer. "Hoody-do!" A crowd of well-wishers surged forward to congratulate him.

"A real nut case. Incredible!" Steve said out loud to himself. But what was so incredible? He'd voted for George himself. After all, reproduction rights was a powerful issue.

George's lips were parted in ecstasy and a rosy glow animated his pale face. From somewhere behind him, perhaps the chemistry sink, he distinctly heard Lauren laughing with delight at his victory, but he kept news of her delicious pealing voice to himself.

"A great moment for English at Muni. I'll try to work speedily and justify your enormous faith in me, for 'FAITH WITHOUT WORKS IS DEAD.'" George gave his supporters a benedictory glance. "A few immediate suggestions—a bulletin board in the corridor outside the English office. Each member of the department will have his own space. I've measured the wall and I calculate that each member including part-timers and graduate assistants will have a six-inch-by-ten-inch spot. Put up anything you like in it—express your inner self. A literary quotation, a baby picture, your latest book jacket, dried flower arrangements.

"Also, through a connection I have with a travel agent in Dublin, I believe we can arrange a charter trip to the Aran Islands and the West Coast at a very cheap cost for the entire department, meals and after-meal entertainment, accordion players, jugglers, clog dancing, etc., included. Next semester I'll get space in the student union for collegewide poetry slams, and for bonding let's try weekly readings from private departmental diaries and journals."

He turned to the milling, gesticulating figures of his dazed supporters, evoking an even greater buzz of enthusiasm. At the same time across the aisle, a small disgruntled group discussed impeachment proceedings in loud voices. The Chair and Quinton packed up and went home, but Allen, Cherry, and Daphne gathered close together. They stopped a moment to listen to George and wince.

". . . followed by low-fat vegetarian dinners for those who care for that sort of thing and drinking parties for those who prefer traditional fun."

"Don't ask why I wanted to upgrade the department," Allen said in a disgusted voice. "I've had offers elsewhere—good ones. Hawaii, California, Michigan." With a shrug, he, too, made for the door.

Meanwhile Mary Burnson had slipped through the crowd to stand proudly at George's side. "Yes, and how about bus trips in the summer months to Walt Whitman's home and other literary sites in the metropolitan area?"

"Sounds a little boring, a little ho-hum, Mary, but I'm sure we can come up with something exciting to do on buses."

Ramona, who'd raced over from Temp 6 to hear the election results, elbowed Mary to reach George's side. Her tiny figure only came up to the zip on his windbreaker.

"Professor Reilly, I'm delighted." She gripped his hand warmly. "I'll help you redecorate the English office with potted plants and posters, as you suggested."

"Bright colors? Easy chairs and ottomans?"

"Whatever," she said with a loving look.

"A cauldron of hot chicken soup on the boil in the English office on wintry days?"

"Of course. With my mum's egg noodle recipe."

George put one arm around Ramona and the other around Mary, and stood easily, though a little lopsidedly. "So kind of you, Ramona. You know nowadays I suffer from memory lapses and poor concentration. I'll be glad of your continuing help. And you, Mary, will you be my associate chair?"

"Oh, George, I'll work so hard!"

"Go home, all you hardworking teachers. Go home to your families. We'll meet again in a week or two and brainstorm. Let's talk about dropping all prerequisites, a pet project of mine."

George screwed up his face in an effort to think of everything at once. "Yapping administrators, deans and associate deans, I don't see why they need to be informed about any of these changes. They always demand reports and studies. They need sharp blows to the head."

Transfigured with happiness, George's handsome face seemed ten years younger. He looked around for Igor, motioned to Steve and Brian to join him, too. "And now for a celebration. Will the hard core follow me for a little exquisite bazouki music? They don't call me El Diablo for nothing!"

9

Steve was in his mummy cell. Locked away from the world amid the susurrations of the air conditioning, Steve experienced the strange atmosphere of ESF for the last time. He bent over his files, tossing purple-inked poems into the battered metal can. Shakespeare. Yeats. Ishmael Reed. Teaching aids, these faded papers were called.

The news had run like wildfire throughout the department. Lauren's line, the only existing job vacancy in the Department of English, had been awarded by the P & B Committee to the distinguished poet Igor Blavatsky. Tomorrow he would gather up his accordion file and move from the part-timers' kennel in the basement of the library to Steve's tiny office.

Crouching on his hands and knees in front of the filing cabinets, Steve felt a lot like barking but refrained. Don't get maudlin, he told himself. You've been unemployed before. You were out of work for the first twenty-four years of your life. Funny how natural that seemed.

Steve left untouched Brian's papers in the right-hand cabinet, though he wasn't sure if Brian would ever move back to 309. Brian now spoke of leaving the country, teaching English in Sri Lanka. Though he had George's good will and stood a chance of securing Quinton's line in the fall, Brian didn't seem inclined to stay at Muni. He longed for strange odors and tempestuous seas.

A loud clanking in the hall. Steve rushed to the door to summon the cleaning woman. Like a genie she rose behind the tall trash barrel on wheels. "Papers?" she said.

"Boy, do I have papers for you." He grimaced. "I'm leaving, you know. Fired. Cleaning everything out—too much trouble to carry home."

Elisabeth shook her head. "I'm sorry, young gentleman. Others should pay, not you. I will come for your papers. Ten *minuten* or more. You have my respect, Dr. Speck." She trundled away at a smart clip.

In the interval Steve decided to check his mail for the last time. He felt chilled, lightheaded. He needed the exercise.

Steve exited ESF just in time to hear squealing brakes and see a near head-on collision between Cherry's blue Honda and a pickup truck with two men and a dog in the cab. Neither had given way in the narrow alley between ESF and Temp 6.

"Watch it, pretty lady!" the bearded driver yelled. "You're supposed to yield!"

"Your mama!" Cherry screamed.

Steve waved his long arms in the air.

"Oh, hi." Cherry backed up a few feet and smiled, ignoring the truck. "Done for the term?"

"For the lifetime," Steve replied. "And you?"

"You're lucky to be leaving this dump. I'm stuck here for two more years."

"How so?"

The truck ahead of them began honking rhythmically, a loud Canadian goose.

"Crostini in comp lit gave me a visiting lectureship. Gives me time to finish my book. Can't wait to lock horns with Fatwood and the English department when she arrives. That'll be fun."

Now the truck honk was continuous and frenzied. "Know of any jobs, Cherry?"

"Nope. Want a lift to the city?"

With the truck blasting and the dog barking, Steve's head was pounding. "Can't go this minute. I have just fifteen, twenty minutes of cleaning up to do."

"Too bad. Keep in touch." Cherry backed up to the parking bay, turned, then sped away in the opposite direction.

When the truck passed by, the two men in the cab gave Steve dirty looks. "Whatsa matter? She on the rag?"

Steve made a horrified face and bolted away.

In the English office, two more workmen were hoisting up the old ditto machine on a dolly, supervised at a little distance by Ramona. She didn't acknowledge Steve as he scurried past to the mail closet, unless by her sniff in the air as if she smelled a bad odor.

The mailbox was stuffed with the usual departmental detritus. A Federal Express envelope contained a student essay accompanied by a note on purple paper smelling faintly of lavender.

> Professor Speck: I know you said you wouldn't accept any late papers, but I was up for a part in a soap and since my entire future acting career depended on it, I had to prepare. Hoping you'll understand, since you've always been a wonderful and kind teacher, Dawn St. John (Dershowitz)

But Steve had handed in his final grades that morning.

Around the corner, Steve heard Ramona scolding an English major. "Your request is very irregular, unheard of. I'll have to ask the new Chair when he gets back from Las Vegas."

Jammed beneath the fat sheaf of papers, ancient minutes of forgotten department meetings, warnings of library closings, threats from the registrar, and exhortations from the dean of faculty, one communique now held Steve's attention.

FROM: Hubert Rosa
           Assistant Dean
           Faculty Support Services
TO: Steven Speck

Persons not reappointed for the following year are obliged to return the following keys no later than June 1:

Men's Humanities Toilet Facility

ESF 309

Library Stack Security Bypass

Keys not returned will be assessed a ten-dollar charge each. No exceptions will be made.

Grunting, Steve took hold of the whole mass of papers and dumped them into the corner trash can. Brushing past the workmen who were still trying to maneuver the unwieldy machine, he broke into a run the moment he left the English department. Legs pumping, he shot out the door of Temp 6 and raced at top speed along the passage to ESF, encountering not a single soul on the way, unless you count Lucille Streng driving past in her white 1980 Volvo. She appeared not to see Steve and narrowly missed running him down.

Captain Jack was sitting in his usual seat in the vestibule of ESF, his rheumy eyes fixed on the revolving door. "Whoa, there, Dr. Speck. You'll give yourself a heart attack running like that. That's the kind of thing I see students do, not perfessors."

Steve paused, panting. "Last time you'll see me do it. Today's my last day on campus."

"I'm right sorry to hear that." Captain Jack stiffly rose to his feet and stuck out his gnarled hand. "We'll miss you. Best of luck and happiness."

"Same to you, Captain Jack."

Steve took the stairs at a more sedate pace to find Elisabeth Hofrichter waiting.

"Everything in order to make am I here," she said with a soldierly nod.

Steve threw the door wide open and propped it there with his briefcase. "You can take everything in that can there, and here, this file, too. Everything in it you can dump. *Alles*. Have fun."

He fell to cleaning out his desk. Now his pace of work was very slow. Why rush home? His apartment was empty. Aimee had gone to London, after all, to study drama. After her escapade with George, her relationship with Steve had blown away and burst like a bubble in the wind.

Steve sighed and popped an old honey menthol cough drop he found in the center drawer into his mouth. "Yugh," he said, spitting it out again onto the desktop. Then he picked up his eight-by-twelve photo of Henry Martin from the bottom drawer and stared at it sullenly.

Sitting at a cluttered Victorian desk, hand propped under his chin, Martin stared back with large dream-struck eyes. "It's a fiasco for you, too, old boy," Steve told him.

As the cleaning woman turned, she caught sight of the portrait of Henry Martin in Steve's hand.

"*Grossvater*!" she shrieked, laying her rough hands on Steve's arm. She tried to pry the photo out of Steve's hand.

"Heinrich Martin," she shrieked again. "*Genie, Dichter, Grossvater*!"

Steve was dumbfounded, hardly able to speak. "This man here in the photo is your grandfather?"

She nodded vigorously. "All his poem to *Grossmutter* habe I in my box. Full of *Liebe—liebevoll*. I show them. Forty, fifty. *Wunderbar*. You will read them, no?"

If there had been windows in ESF, someone looking in might have seen Steve Speck, lecturer in English, leap up to embrace the maintenance person. Steve, for his part, might have peered out to see the departmental ditto machine making its slow way across campus on a truck, heading for a new life in the English-as-a-second-language division.

In the distance, the flag in the center of the quad whipped bravely in the wind.